'Those are my terms, Boyd.'

'Terms? Is this war, then?' He was glaring at Clare across the table. 'I knew something like this was going to happen. I was right when I said you've changed.'

'If you mean that I've decided to take control of my own life, then yes, I have changed.'

'And what about me?'

'If you love me you won't try to stop me.'

Dear Reader

Autumn's here and the nights are drawing in—but when better to settle down with your favourite romances? This month, Mills & Boon have made sure that you won't notice the colder weather—our wide range of love stories are sure to warm the chilliest of hearts! Whether you're wanting a rattling good read, something sweet and magical, or to be carried off to hot, sunny countries—like Australia, Greece or Venezuela—we've got the books to please you.

Enjoy!

The Editor

Sally Wentworth was born and raised in Hertfordshire, where she still lives, and started writing after attending an evening-class course. She is married and has one son and a dog—a Great Dane. There is always a novel on the bedside table, but she also does craftwork, plays bridge, ar.d is the president of a National Trust group. They go to the ballet and theatre regularly and open-air concerts in the summer. Sometimes she doesn't know how she finds the time to write!

Recent titles by the same author:

THE GOLDEN GREEK
STORMY VOYAGE

THE
WAYWARD WIFE

BY

SALLY WENTWORTH

MILLS & BOON LIMITED
ETON HOUSE   18-24 PARADISE ROAD
RICHMOND   SURREY   TW9 1SR

First published in Great Britain 1992
by Mills & Boon Limited

© Sally Wentworth 1992

Australian copyright 1992
Philippine copyright 1992
This edition 1992

ISBN 0 263 77791 X

Set in Times Roman 10 on 11½ pt.
01-9211-55703 C

Made and printed in Great Britain

CHAPTER ONE

THE phone rang, breaking through the soft background music from the cassette player, breaking through Clare's deep concentration as she worked at the big table set beneath the window. After three rings the answer-phone cut in and she carried on working, adding delicate brush strokes to the picture of a horse she was painting. The phone immediately rang again, but again she ignored it, trying to shut it out. When, only a few moments later, the strident tone filled the room for a third time, she knew that there was only one person it could be.

'Hell!' Clare threw down her brush in annoyance, turned off the music and picked up the phone. 'Now what?' she demanded angrily.

'And hello to you, darling,' Boyd said sardonically. 'Supposing I'd been a customer?'

'A customer would have realised that I'm working and would have had the courtesy to leave a message rather than disturb me.'

'Well, I'm a husband and I'm privileged.'

'I could think of a more apt word,' Clare retorted, still angry. 'What is it this time?'

Boyd's tone hardened. 'A Polish buyer has arrived in England a week early and brought his wife with him. She wants to——'

'No,' Clare cut in before he could go any further. 'I'm not trailing round the West End with a woman I don't know and whose language I don't speak. Get one of your secretaries to do it.'

5

'Clare, the man is an up-and-coming businessman in a new regime; exactly the right person we've been looking for to break into that area of the East European market. The company wants to make them feel especially welcome and give——'

'You don't have to spell it out; I think I may just have heard it all once or twice before. You know I have this calendar commission to finish, Boyd; they want it by the end of the month.'

'They can wait a couple more days, surely?'

'That's hardly a professional attitude. Would you keep your Polish customer hanging around a couple of days? This is a new outlet and the publisher might not give me any more work if I'm late.'

'Look,' Boyd's tone became more persuasive, 'this is important to me, Clare.'

'So is my work to me.'

'I know that—believe me, I know it.' He paused for a moment and she could imagine him gritting his teeth, trying to suppress his anger. 'But you know I'm in the running for the sales director's job, and we agreed that you'd give me one hundred per cent support.'

'No, that's what you decided,' Clare said shortly. 'I don't remember being given a vote.'

Boyd lowered his voice, but his tone grew sharp. 'I'm not going to argue with you over the phone, Clare. Just remember that I earn the money we live on, that pays the mortgage. I want you available tomorrow to take my customer's wife wherever she wants to go, and I want you here in London by seven-thirty tonight when I take them out to dinner.'

'Tonight as well!' Clare wailed. 'That isn't fair; I'll have to start getting ready now to be there on time.'

'You were the one who wanted to move out to the country,' Boyd pointed out acidly. 'Be here.' And he put the phone down.

Clare almost rebelled, but it was always almost. No matter how angry she became, she had never let Boyd down yet, and he shamelessly took advantage of the fact. Looking first at her watch and then in the mirror, Clare wondered if she could get away with not washing her hair, which would give her another half an hour in which to work, but then she gave an angry sigh; if she was going to be in London all day tomorrow then it would have to be washed today. Feeling bitter with resentment, she carefully washed her brushes and tidied her work table, then ran upstairs to get ready.

Boyd had a company car and drove up to town every day, and Clare had a much smaller and older car, but she took a taxi to the station in the nearby market town and caught a train up to Kings Cross, then took the Underground to the station nearest to Boyd's office. Most of the commuters had gone home by now and the dark streets were almost empty, although there were lights in nearly all the buildings, most of them modern office blocks that had been built during the boom years of the past decade. Boyd's company owned a whole building, Chilton House, very late twentieth century, still ablaze with lights on all of its twelve floors. Boyd's office was on the eighth floor. If he got the promotion to sales director he would then have a seat on the board and would move up to the tenth floor. Moving up in every way, Clare thought cynically as she pushed open the heavy glass door and walked in.

'Hello, Ken.'

The night security man gave her a beaming smile. 'Evening, Mrs Russell. Another night out on the tiles? It's all right for some.' But there was no envy in his voice.

They had known each other for over eight years, ever since Clare had started going out with Boyd, and she knew all about his family, his son who was a policeman, and his two little granddaughters. Picking up the phone, he rang through to Boyd's office to tell him she'd arrived.

Clare opened her bag and took out an envelope. 'A little Christmas present for your grandchildren,' she said lightly.

Inside were two tiny pictures of mice in their nests that she'd painted to hang on the walls of the girls' doll's house. 'They'll love them,' he said with delight. 'You've put such a lot of detail in them, too,' he added, putting on his glasses to see better. 'It's very kind of you; you shouldn't have gone to all that trouble.'

'I enjoyed it.' She glanced towards the lifts as the signal pinged and the doors of one of them began to open. Boyd stepped out, looking as immaculate as he had when he'd left home that morning—but then he always did. Tall, and with dark hair that grew in unruly curls, he had an air of youthful vitality and enthusiasm that masked his overriding ambition. His hazel eyes, under dark, straight brows, were bright and humorous, as if he got a great deal of fun out of life. His lips were wide and quirked a little, always ready to smile. It was only the strong thrust of his jaw that gave any hint of the determination to succeed that had carried him so far up the career ladder in such a short time. That and his charm, of course, because Boyd had an abundance of that, which came to him quite naturally, but which he could also use as a weapon, with deadly effect.

'Darling.' He came over to put a possessive hand on her arm, but he only kissed her lightly on the cheek, then looked her over, checking that she was smartly dressed, that she wouldn't let him down. Clare gave him an old-fashioned look, her eyes speaking volumes, and he said, 'Glad you could make it,' with a faint hint of sardonic triumph.

They said goodnight to Ken and went down to the underground car park to get Boyd's car, a Rover. 'We're to pick up the Prizbilskis at their hotel,' he told her as they drove away. 'Then we're going on to a Chinese restaurant.'

'Are they very old?'

'No, not really. Fiftyish.'

'They're old,' Clare said with foreboding. 'What on earth am I supposed to talk to the wife about? We'll have nothing in common. This whole thing is ridiculous.'

'Why don't you tell her about your work?' Boyd suggested shortly. 'It's all you seem interested in nowadays.'

'Look, I came, didn't I?' she snapped out, angrily turning to face him.

He glanced at her, then put out a hand to briefly cover and squeeze hers. 'I know. Sorry. Look, it can't be helped, so let's try and enjoy tonight, OK? At least we'll be together. Surely that's better than me entertaining them alone?'

'Yes, I suppose so.' But Clare gave a long sigh.

Hearing it, Boyd grew angry again. 'Don't go overboard with enthusiasm,' he said curtly.

Clare looked at his lean profile for a moment, then leaned back in her seat, relaxing for the first time. 'It's just that I'd much rather have spent the evening at home together, that's all. We seem to have had so little time there since we moved in.'

The wistful note in her voice made him say hearteningly, 'Never mind, I'll be home this weekend.'

But I'll have to work this weekend if I want to get those calendar illustrations finished in time, Clare thought bitterly. She almost said it aloud, but stopped herself, and after a moment said, 'Promise?'

'Definitely.'

Leaning across, she kissed him on his cheek. 'Good.'

Boyd grinned, his mood happy again. But then, he was always happy so long as he got his own way.

The Prizbilskis were waiting in the foyer of their hotel, eager for their evening out in London. Clare was relieved to find that they both spoke passable English. In fact, they were both much nicer than she'd expected and so full of praise and delight in everything they saw that she couldn't fail to like them. Clare was used to having to act as escort to the wives of Boyd's customers from more sophisticated countries, women who wanted to be taken round Harrods, chic clothes shops in Chelsea, or to Bond Street auction houses to bid for antiques. So when she asked Mrs Prizbilski what she would like to do tomorrow and the lady said confidingly, 'I have heard so much about your Marks & Spencers; could we go there?' Clare was enchanted and said warmly,

'Of course. We'll go wherever you want.'

It was almost eleven before they took their guests back to their hotel and were able to set out for home. 'Well, wasn't so bad, was it?' Boyd remarked.

'No, they were nice. So eager to be pleased with everything. I wish they were all like that. Do you think you'll do business with them?'

'No reason why not if we can reach a financial agreement.'

'And the company makes enough profit, of course,' Clare said on a scornful note.

'Profit is what the shareholders want, what we're paid to produce,' Boyd reminded her, his tone less acid than it might have been.

Clare looked moodily out of the window. 'Sure, the fast buck, the six-monthly dividend. That's what it's all about.'

'You speak as though profit has suddenly become a dirty word. You didn't used to feel that way.'

'No, I know.' She stared out of the window, blindly watching the endless procession of sodium lamp-posts, their light taking sickly orange bites out of the darkness of the night. It was true, Clare thought; when they'd met and when they'd married, over seven years ago, she had been as keen and as ambitious as Boyd. She could remember having champagne dinners to celebrate whenever he was promoted, got a rise, or achieved a sales target. She had been thrilled and delighted at his rapid rise through Chilton House, happy that his superiors had recognised the potential that she had always known he had: his flair, his acute business sense, and his ability to charm the customers, especially the female clients, of which there seemed to be an ever-growing number nowadays.

And she, too, had been successful on a humbler scale, working as a graphic artist for an advertising company. Her work had been good and she'd been head-hunted to a bigger company at about the same time as Boyd had got a rise, so they'd taken on a huge mortgage and gone in for a decent Georgian town house in Fulham, moving from their cramped flat in an old house in Hackney. Life had been great then for a while, they'd widened their circle of friends and done a lot of entertaining, the only drawback being that Boyd had to go away such a lot to trade fairs and on sales trips. Clare missed him while he was away but wasn't lonely because she had her work and her circle of friends. But after a year or so she'd begun to get restless, feeling that something was missing in her life, but hadn't realised what it was until a close friend had had her first baby. I'm getting broody, she'd thought, stunned by the revelation, and rather amused by it. She'd told Boyd of her feelings and they'd both laughed, convinced it was only a temporary aberration. But the feeling hadn't gone away and it had led to nothing but unhappiness.

'Asleep?' Boyd asked softly, breaking into her reverie.

Clare stirred and turned her head to face the road again. 'No, just thinking.'

He didn't have to ask what about; the heaviness in her tone gave her away. Reaching out, he covered her hand again. 'Soon be home,' he said comfortingly.

Home was a sprawling old farmhouse on the edge of an equally old and quaint village, a place that town people could drive out to on a Sunday to stroll round and have a drink in the village pub. Far enough away from London to feel rural but within an easy distance for the drive back. And so within the commuter belt. Boyd turned into their gateway and pulled up in front of the garage. There was frost on the door as Clare pushed it open, and she hurried inside the house, glad of the centrally heated warmth, but wishing there was a fire waiting for them in the inglenook fireplace in the sitting-room. But it was too late to light one now, gone midnight.

Clare took off her jacket and dropped it on a chair just as Boyd came in. He glanced at her but then his eyes lingered on her slim figure as she reached up to take the clips out of her hair and let its rich chestnut fullness fall loose on her shoulders. Coming over to her, he put his hands on her waist, his fingers almost meeting, and drew her to him. 'How come I still only have to look at you to turn me on?' he murmured against her hair.

'Because you're an insatiable sex-maniac and I'm the only woman fool enough to put up with you, that's why,' Clare answered flippantly.

He held her against his hardening body. 'Do I still turn you on?' he asked softly, raising his head to look in her eyes.

Clare's lips parted a little and her voice grew husky as she put her hands on his shoulders. 'Let's find out, shall we?'

Next morning was the usual rush when they were both going out at the same time, although Boyd got to the bathroom first again, as usual. He always left early, before the rush-hour jams got too bad, and it was easier for Clare to travel up with him, even though she would be too early to collect Mrs Prizbilski from her hotel.

Boyd started making calls on the car phone almost as soon as they left the house. It would have been easier for Clare to drive and him to use the phone, but Boyd preferred to drive himself; and he was a good driver, always seeing the gaps in the traffic that shortened the journey by ten minutes or so. He would have made a good rally driver; it was part of his nature to win, to make a competition out of just this daily drive. To turn the car into a racing office, Clare thought wryly as he accelerated into the fast lane.

When they arrived at Chilton House it was still before eight-thirty. Clare went up to his office with Boyd to have a coffee before she collected Mrs Prizbilski. Usually he was the only one in the department this early, and she had to make the coffee herself, but today one of his secretaries had already arrived and was seated at her desk in the big outer office. It was a new girl, one Clare hadn't seen before. She smiled as she saw Boyd and got quickly to her feet, the smile slipping a little when she saw Clare behind him.

'Good morning, Velma. Can you rustle up a couple of coffees for my wife and me?'

'Of course.' The girl was wearing a short, tight-fitting black dress and had very light blonde hair.

Clare watched her go and said, 'Can she type as well?'

'As well as what?' Boyd ushered her into his own office and shut the door. Clare merely raised her eyebrows at him and he grinned. 'I haven't had to complain yet.'

'About the typing?'

After taking her coat from her Boyd put his arm round her waist. 'Your eyes always go a darker green when you're jealous,' he remarked complacently.

'I'm not jealous. Did you choose her?'

'You *are* jealous. No, the personnel department did.'

'No, I'm not. Just don't come home with any blonde hairs on your jacket, that's all.'

Boyd laughed. His eyes softened and he kissed her lightly. 'After a night like last night, do you really think that I even want to look at another woman?'

He moved away as his phone rang, and Clare went to sit on a chair placed at right-angles to the window, but instead of looking out she watched her husband as he dealt quickly and efficiently with the caller. She hadn't answered his question, but then, she didn't have to. She might put on an act of being jealous but she had never had any reason to be, even though Boyd was often away from home. His work took the place of 'the other woman', making constant demands on his time and energy, although he always seemed to have enough energy for sex and was a very accomplished lover. Clare smiled to herself, thinking that if degrees were ever to be awarded for sexual prowess Boyd would definitely be a Master of the Art—or would the title be Master of the Bedchamber?

'You've got your contented-cat look.' Boyd had put down the phone and was watching her. 'Now what can you be thinking about, I wonder?'

She didn't answer, just tilted her head slightly to one side and looked at him under her lashes. He smiled broadly. 'Temptress.' He came over and put his hands on the arms of her chair and bent to kiss her.

'Sex-maniac.' Lifting her arms, she put them round his neck.

There was a brief knock and the secretary came in with the coffees. Boyd didn't jerk away, instead leisurely finishing the kiss and laughing into Clare's eyes before he straightened up.

'Thanks, Velma.' The girl walked out of the office, her cheeks a little flushed, her face set. Boyd grinned. 'You timed that very well.'

'*I* didn't do anything.' Getting to her feet, Clare walked over to get her coffee. She had dressed down a little today, not wanting to create too big a gap between herself and her Polish guest, and was wearing a deep red dress left over from her working career. But the colour suited her, emphasising the fragile delicacy of her high cheekbones and straight nose, and the warmth of her mouth, a mouth that was used to smiling. Almost three years old, the dress was longer than current fashions and hid a pair of very shapely legs, now thrust into sensible low-heeled boots for a day's shopping.

Boyd became busy on the phone again, confirming arrangements for a trade fair in Bruges next spring. After drinking her coffee Clare sat on until it was time to go. She mouthed 'Goodbye' to Boyd, who was on the phone again.

Covering the receiver, he said, 'Meet you here at six. We'll eat in town rather than wait till we get home.'

It wasn't what Clare wanted, but she nodded and said, 'Yes. OK.' Then lifted a hand in farewell.

It was a long, tiring day. Mrs Prizbilski had a three-page-long list of things she wanted to buy, not only for herself but also for every member of her family and every neighbour and friend she had ever made. Or so it seemed as Clare patiently led her from department store to department store along Oxford Street while she tried to choose what she wanted. 'Do you think this will be right for my cousin's grandchild?' was the sort of question she had to try to answer. Clare was thankful when the stores closed at five-thirty and she was able to drop off her guest and go back to Boyd's office, but even then she couldn't relax because they were joined for dinner by some of his colleagues, both male and female, who talked shop all through the meal.

Clare could feel herself getting uptight as they talked, these upwardly mobile and very sophisticated young people, motivated by ambition, and each of them wondering who would get Boyd's job if he was promoted to sales director. His recommendation would, of course, be vitally important, but that wasn't the reason that they listened to his opinions and theories so attentively; Boyd was more than good at his job and they were greedy to learn from him. 'If you're not well on the road to where you want to be by the time you're thirty, you might as well give up,' he was saying now.

'Just so long as the road isn't going in the wrong direction,' Clare put in drily.

Boyd glanced at her and his mouth twisted into a wry grin. 'My wife has worked harder for the company today than any of us, and I think it's about time I took her home.'

'Did you have to put the blame for breaking up the party on me?' Clare asked tersely after they'd left the restaurant and were in the car, driving home.

'It was what you wanted, wasn't it?'

'Yes, but you could have said that *you* were ready to leave.'

'Hell, Clare, does it matter?'

'Yes, it does; now they'll think I'm just a killjoy.'

'Well, aren't you?' he said irritably.

'Oh, thanks a million!' Clare exclaimed. 'I've given up a day and a half to your damn company and that's all the thanks I get.'

'I don't ask any more of you than any of the directors ask of their wives.'

'Like hell! I don't see the managing director's wife just dropping everything to escort a complete stranger around London.'

'She's always on hand when necessary; you see her at the Christmas dinners, don't you?'

Clare fell silent, knowing that she could never win in an argument with him. 'OK. I'm sorry,' she said after a few moments. 'I guess I resent the demands the company makes on your time—and on mine.'

'I'm grateful, darling, believe me. In the present economic climate it's a rat race out there, you know, trying to get orders. We have to do everything we can to swing it our way.'

She nodded, a little mollified. 'At least we'll have the weekend in peace,' she said with a sigh. 'We can look foward to that.'

Boyd was silent for a long time, then said, 'Clare,' in a tone she recognised.

Turning to look at him apprehensively, she said, 'What have you done?'

'The Prizbilskis will be in London over the weekend and they don't know anyone, so——'

'You haven't?' Clare said through gritted teeth.

'Not the whole weekend,' Boyd said hastily. 'Just Sunday.'

'Boyd, I could *kill* you. We agreed never to let work interfere with our Sundays together. You know that.'

'I felt sorry for them,' he said defensively. 'They had nowhere to go.'

'Rubbish! All the galleries, museums and cinemas are open on Sundays; they could have found plenty to do. Why don't you tell the truth—you haven't clinched the deal yet, have you? Well?' she insisted when he didn't answer. 'That's the true reason, isn't it?'

'All right, maybe that's part of it, but they wanted to see an English home. Prizbilski was dropping hints all day. It would have been churlish not to invite them.' He pulled off the road into their driveway. 'I thought you wouldn't mind so much. I thought you liked them.'

'I do,' Clare admitted in a tight voice. 'But I love *you* and I wanted to be with you. And you promised that we'd have this weekend.' Pushing open the door, she got out of the car and hurried into the house. It was too late to light a fire again, too late to relax together and listen to some music. Clare went straight upstairs without waiting for Boyd to come in. She ran a bath and went back in the bedroom to take off her clothes. She had got as far as her slip and was hanging her dress in the wardrobe when Boyd came into the room.

He came up behind her. 'How about me taking the rest off?' he said suggestively, and put his hands on her shoulders.

Clare shook him off. 'I'm just a tired old killjoy, remember?' Going into the bathroom, she shut the door firmly behind her but didn't bolt it; she never had since they'd been married. Boyd had insisted on a bath big enough to hold the two of them comfortably and they often shared it, and that of course had often led to the most sensational lovemaking. But tonight Clare was in no mood for love; she just wanted to relax and let the stress and tension float away.

Lying in the bath, she closed her eyes, trying not to think about today, or about their lost weekend. Am I a killjoy? she asked herself. Maybe she was. Once she would probably have enjoyed that meal with the others, would have joined in instead of sitting almost silently as if they were all talking a foreign language. But tonight all she had wanted was for it to end so she and Boyd could go home. Her values had changed, she realised. And she had changed, too, become a different person, who looked back on her old life with a kind of impatient pity. But Boyd hadn't changed. Even though he had gone through the last two traumatic years with her, it hadn't changed him. If anything, he had turned even more to his work, become even more ambitious.

But then, Boyd had never been particularly paternal, although it had been an accepted thing between them when they'd got married that some day they would probably have children. But the 'some day' had been in the far-distant future until she had started getting broody. Boyd hadn't wanted a child then; he'd said the mortgage was too high for just his salary and they ought to wait. So she'd waited, for six months, then conveniently forgotten to take the Pill until she got pregnant. Which hadn't taken long; Boyd was so virile that if she hadn't been taking the Pill during their marriage she would probably have got pregnant at the drop of a hat.

She had been so happy, so over the moon. Boyd had opened his mouth to deliver an angry reproof, but her radiant face had stopped him. Instead he'd said with heavy irony, 'I thought it took two.'

'Oh, it did. It did.' Clare had sat on his lap and kissed and cajoled him into a happier mood. She was full of plans; she would take on free-lance work at home to help pay the mortgage. Everything would work out and life would be just wonderful—for the three of them. But a couple of months later she'd had the miscarriage, the first miscarriage. Boyd had been sympathetic about her disappointment, but he'd expected her just to forget it and go on as they had before.

Clare did her best to forget, but she got depressed, and when her doctor advised her to try again she'd leapt at the idea because in her heart that was what she'd wanted. Having overridden Boyd's objections once, it was easy to do so again, but the disappointment had been doubly hard when she'd had the second miscarriage after three months.

Clare shivered suddenly, realising that the water had gone cold. She stood up just as Boyd banged on the door. 'You about finished in there?'

'Two minutes.'

Picking up a bath sheet, Clare quickly dried herself and wrapped it round her, then shook her hair free of the clips she'd used to keep it out of the water. 'OK. You can come in.'

Boyd's eyebrows rose when he saw the bath towel. 'Don't you want me to dry your back?'

'No, I managed.'

'Little Miss Prim tonight, are we?'

She didn't answer and he went over to the hand-basin to clean his teeth. Clare took the opportunity to go into the bedroom and slip into her nightdress, a white cotton one rather than the kind of silky négligé that Boyd liked. When he came out of the bathroom she was already in bed, her bedside lamp turned off. Boyd never wore pyjamas. He took off his towelling robe and climbed into bed beside her, turning off the lamp on his bedside table.

The darkness was welcome, a mental relief. Clare closed her eyes, but then stiffened as she felt Boyd reach for her. 'It's all right,' he soothed, and drew her into the shelter of his arms, her body curved against his, encompassed by him. He stroked her hair from her face, his hand gentle, and kissed her neck a couple of times, but when she didn't respond he lowered his hand and let his arm lie across her waist. Slowly Clare relaxed. What's the matter with me? she wondered unhappily. Why is it that I wanted sex last night but I don't want it tonight? No wonder Boyd gets mad with me sometimes.

She sighed and Boyd's arms tightened for a moment. 'Go to sleep, Miss Prim,' he murmured in her ear.

He fell asleep himself almost immediately, his relaxed breath disturbing her hair. Clare expected to fall asleep at once herself, but annoyingly found herself unable to. She closed her eyes firmly against her thoughts, but her mind betrayed her every time, bringing her back to the sharpness of reality. I ought to be over it by now, she thought unhappily. I've just got to face the fact that I'll probably never be able to have a child, never hold my baby in my arms. Her heart filled with unconsolable sadness and Clare had to fight back tears, knowing that if she cried she would wake Boyd. He hated to see her cry. It upset him and he got impatient sometimes because there seemed to be nothing he could do to comfort her. He wasn't good at handling sickness, although he had been wonderful when she'd had to spend all those weeks in hospital and then home in bed when she'd been pregnant for the third time. The last time. The doctors had advised against going in for another baby, and Boyd had made it very clear that they weren't going through all that again.

Clare dozed fitfully and came fully awake to see by the luminous dial of the clock that it was still only two-thirty. Giving up trying to sleep, she carefully slipped out of bed and groped for her housecoat and slippers in

the dark, not putting them on until she was outside the
door. The central heating had gone off at midnight and
the house felt chill, but there was an electric fire in the
room she grandly called her studio. Her work was as
she'd left it so abruptly two days before. Pulling the fire
nearer, Clare sat down and, with a small sigh of satisfaction, began to paint.

At five-thirty she tore herself away from her work and
crawled back into bed, the sheets on her half cold to her
skin. Boyd stirred a little and she held her breath, but
he didn't wake. Satisfied, Clare moved nearer to him,
grateful for his warmth, and fell instantly asleep.

Only an hour or so later he woke her with his kisses,
warm on her mouth, and made love to her while she was
still half asleep. Her body responded of its own accord,
arching towards him, moving with sensuous delight to
his expertise. Afterwards she opened languid eyes. 'I
ought to be angry with you.'

He grinned at her, his mouth curved in triumphant
amusement. 'I wonder why you're not. Could it be that
you enjoyed it?'

'You know I did. I always do.' There was a note of
almost guilty regret in her voice that made him laugh.

Boyd pushed himself off her and got out of bed, whis-
tling as he used the bathroom and got dressed. 'Bye,
darling. Go back to sleep,' he said as he came over and
kissed her goodbye.

Fat chance, Clare thought, but without resentment.
She heard him go downstairs and she could imagine him
pouring himself an orange juice as he listened to the
early-morning news on the radio. That drunk, he would
collect his things and go, sometimes even remembering
to close the door quietly on the way out. The sound of
the Rover's engine broke the morning stillness, got louder

as he drove past the house, then died as he accelerated down the road.

Clare turned over and tried to go to sleep again but knew that she wouldn't, although making love had drained her strength and she didn't feel like getting up either. Mentally awake but physically exhausted. She thought with pleasure of having the day to herself, to work on the calendar, but then remembered that it was Friday and Boyd had invited their Polish guests for Sunday. That meant that she would have to do the shopping and clean the house today; Boyd didn't like her doing that kind of thing when he was home. Selfish swine, she thought with a flash of resentment. He'd used to help, though, when they'd lived in London and she'd been working full-time, but once they'd moved to the country and she had given up her job he had expected her to do all the housework while he was at work. Clare had tried pointing out that she was trying to build up a free-lance business but he had just shrugged and said she might just as well go back to her old job and earn some real money.

Forcing herself to get up, Clara showered, then rushed around with dusters and vacuum cleaner, 'tarting the place up', as she called it. That done, she skipped lunch and got out the car to drive to the nearest town, where she stood in line at the bank, the fishmonger's, the baker's, the supermarket check-out. Then home to put the shopping away and grab a couple of hours in which to work before it was time to start cooking dinner.

Sometimes on Saturdays Boyd went out to the local country club to play squash or golf, but this week he had nothing arranged, so they went to an antiques fair. Clare couldn't complain; she had passed her own growing love of antiques on to Boyd, and they had enjoyed buying pieces of furniture from sales, renovating them, and putting them in the house. It was one of the few things he had come to enjoy about living in the country, so Clare had always been keen to encourage it. They had lunch out and went on to a town that was noted for its number of antiques shops. Usually she enjoyed wandering round them, but today she had to hide her impatience, wishing she were home. Not that she could hide it completely; Boyd knew her too well for that, and she was almost sure he was deliberately taking his time.

In the evening they went out to dinner with some friends and didn't get home until the early hours. But again Clare sneaked downstairs to do some work.

On Sunday morning Boyd had to drive up to London to collect the Prizbilskis while Clare started cooking the dinner. She was giving them traditional English roast beef and Yorkshire pudding, keeping her fingers crossed that the latter would come out OK, because she was no expert as a cook. As always, their guests were pleased and grateful, often repeating their thanks, and luckily the pudding had risen as it should. After lunch the sun came out and they took the Polish couple for a walk round the village, which, with its old Tudor houses and small river running through its centre, was very picturesque.

Boyd walked ahead with Mr Prizbilski while Clare followed more slowly with his wife. 'You look tired,' the older woman remarked as Clare stifled a yawn. 'I hope we have not been too much trouble for you.'

'No, of course not,' Clare smiled. 'Sometimes I don't sleep very well, that's all.'

Her guest gave her a shrewd glance. 'You have no children?' Clare shook her head silently. 'Perhaps you have not been married for many years?'

'Seven.'

'You do not wish for children?' Mrs Prizbilski asked with all the inquisitiveness of a woman with three children and several grandchildren.

Clare fought the desire to tell her to mind her own business, but then said, 'Yes, I want children very much.'

'This is a good place for children.' Her companion nodded, looking round.

'Yes, that's what I thought, but I—but I can't have any.' Clare saw the sympathy in the other woman's eyes, and suddenly she was pouring it all out to this complete stranger. About her two miscarriages in London and her fears that it was the exhaust fumes and using a VDU screen a lot that had caused them. How she had begged and pleaded with Boyd to leave London and come here, and had been so full of hope when she had soon become pregnant again. But she had dehydrated and had to go to hospital to be put on a drip and kept there for weeks, then home for more weeks in bed, with her mother looking after her. And back to hospital when she had dehydrated yet again. But it hadn't been any good; all those days of patient hope and longing had been wasted; she had dehydrated too often and had lost the baby. She had come home to Boyd so wretched and depressed that she had agreed when he'd made her promise never to put them through the ordeal again.

The Polish woman's English wasn't good enough for her to have understood all that Clare had blurted out, but she clucked in motherly sympathy and put a pitying hand on her arm. Clare was immediately ashamed of her outburst and afraid that Mrs Prizbilski might say something to Boyd, but luckily she didn't. They stayed to tea and then Boyd drove them back to their hotel, giving Clare a couple of free hours in which to work, but by this time she was so tired that she could hardly concentrate.

It's no good, I'll have to leave it till tomorrow, she thought angrily after she'd made her third mistake. She went upstairs to have a bath, wishing that she were free to lead her own life. The thought brought her up short, made her feel terribly disloyal. She was Boyd's wife, and there was no way she wanted to change that. But resentment filled her again. She might be his wife but she was entitled to a life of her own, and she didn't want to spend that life as Boyd's appendage, his accessory to be taken out and polished up whenever his precious company needed her. She wanted her own life, not to live through him. She loved Boyd but she didn't love the life he was making her lead.

CHAPTER TWO

BOYD got the Polish contract. And he got the promotion to sales director. Whether one led to the other, Clare wasn't sure, but it certainly must have helped. At the end of that week the other directors called him into the boardroom and told him that he was to take over the position on the first of January, when the present sales director retired. That night Boyd came home full of the news, carrying a magnum of champagne to celebrate, and an armful of flowers for Clare. He had sounded the horn in a triumphal blast as he'd turned in the drive and, not bothering to garage the car, ran into the house. 'I've got it!' he yelled as soon as he opened the door.

'Got what?' Clare turned as he burst into the kitchen.

'You are now looking at the new sales director of Chilton House Holdings,' Boyd said exultantly.

'Oh, that.' Clare pretended to be bored. 'About time.' His jaw dropped, but then Clare gave a great yell and ran into his arms. 'That's marvellous! Wonderful.' She hugged him fiercely. 'I just knew you'd get it. You're a genius. They would have been fools not to give it to you.'

Boyd lifted her off her feet and swung her round, the flowers and champagne still in his hands. 'They made quite a thing of it,' he said, still on a high. 'They called me into the boardroom and they were all there, even the old man himself,' he told her, referring to the president of the group of companies. 'They had a couple of bottles of really good vintage wine waiting, and——' he paused to emphasise his next words '—they called me by my first name.'

'Oh, wow!' Clare was suitably impressed. 'And did they give you a key to the directors' cloakroom?'

'The directors have their own cloakrooms. Their offices come *en suite*.' Setting her down on her feet, Boyd laughed at her, his face still alight with excitement. 'These are for you. And there are more in the car.' He gave her the flowers and kissed her. 'Because you helped,' he said generously. 'They specially mentioned how much they appreciated what you'd done for the company.'

Maybe they had, but it was Boyd whom she'd done it for. And it was Boyd who'd worked so hard, so ambitiously, to attain the position. Whether it would mean that he would have to be away at trade fairs and conferences more, she didn't know. Probably. They were hardly likely to have made him a director unless it meant more work, more responsibility. But tonight Clare pushed all thoughts of the future out of her mind. Tonight was Boyd's, they would celebrate and she would make sure that the evening was perfect for him.

They lit the fire in the dining-room and ate by candle-light, the flames reflected in the big mirror on the chimney breast, and off brass and copper, and the old blue and white plates that Clare had collected and hung on the walls. The thick velvet curtains were drawn and the room felt warm and intimate, enclosing them in the soft glow of the candles. For Clare, it was one of the happiest evenings they'd spent together since they had moved into the house. It was the sort of time she had dreamed they would have here but seldom did. Boyd told her everything again in detail, savouring the memory, fixing it in his mind, and Clare listened and questioned in wifely eagerness, sharing it with him, happy that he was so happy.

'They're going to announce the appointment in a couple of weeks,' he told her. 'Just before the Christmas binge.'

The 'Christmas binge' was the company's official annual dinner and dance for all the employees and took place on one of the last Saturdays before Christmas. It was always held at one of the new, plush hotels on the outskirts of London, and wives and husbands, girlfriends and boyfriends were also invited. It was the grand, gala occasion of the year and everyone dressed up to the nines, the women wearing new dresses bought specially for the evening or else old ones that they hoped no one would remember. For the men it was easy; they just wore their dinner-jackets.

The first time Clare had gone to the party she had been just a girlfriend and excited and nervous, not wanting to let Boyd down. She had spent days shopping for a suitable dress, something fashionable but not too way out in case she was introduced to Boyd's boss, but found when she got to the dinner that they were on a table with the rest of the sales-department staff, while the directors and their wives all sat on a top table, separated from everyone else by a barrier of flower arrangements and the space of the dance-floor. Since then Clare had become quite blasé about the occasion, usually enjoying herself when she got there but no longer looking forward to it or feeling at all nervous. The dinner dances had become just another duty evening, but were a good excuse for buying a new dress.

But now, with some misgivings, she said, 'I suppose we'll have to sit at the top table from now on?'

'Not this time; John Broome doesn't retire until the end of the year. And as this will be his last Christmas with the firm they want to make it memorable for him. They've asked me to organise a presentation.'

'Have you anything in mind?'

Boyd, of course, had lots of ideas. They discussed them as they ate their pudding, then took what was left of the champagne into the sitting-room. The fire in this room, too, was ablaze, logs piled on to the grate in the inglenook, giving enough light for them not to need a lamp. They pulled the big, comfortable old settee up in front of it and Boyd put on a tape of his favourite New Orleans jazz music. Clare tucked her feet under her and leaned her head against Boyd's shoulder, feeling happy and content. In the past she had often felt that way, and it occurred to her that this had become almost a strange emotion nowadays, but she pushed the thought resolutely aside, not wanting to spoil the moment.

After refilling their glasses Boyd told her of the financial package he'd been offered with the job. 'Not only do I get a rise in salary and a better car, but I also get a percentage of overall sales and a director's fee.'

'Good heavens, we'll be rich!' Clare exclaimed in awe.

'You certainly won't have to go on working, my darling.' Boyd's hand tightened on her shoulder.

Her not working would, she knew, give him satisfaction. It would be part of his achievement in getting the new job. Few of the other directors' wives worked; but then, they mostly had families to look after.

'I need something to do,' Clare said, her voice tightening.

Boyd sensed it immediately and stroked her arm as he said soothingly, 'Yes, of course. But you could just paint for pleasure, if you wanted to.'

There was no point in trying to explain that she needed a challenge, that she had to have some motivation to occupy the empty hours, to try to fill the vacuum in her life. So she merely held out her glass and said, 'Is there any more of this gorgeous fizz?'

As he leaned back against the settee Boyd's voice grew dreamy as he painted a picture of their possible future. 'You must have a new car; whatever make you like. Perhaps a sports car? And maybe we'll get an apartment in Spain, near a golf course.'

'You don't play golf,' Clare objected.

'No, but I'll probably take it up when I get too old to play squash.'

'How long will that be?'

'Oh, I don't know—another fifteen years or so.' He laughed. 'Maybe we'll forget the apartment. I know, how about a small holiday cottage in France? In Provence? You might be able to paint there. Think of the light. And the flowers. You'd like that, wouldn't you? How about if we take a motoring holiday there next year and have a look round?'

'Sounds fantastic.' Clare nestled closer to him and kissed his neck, then nibbled his earlobe, which she knew always drove him mad.

He stood it for a couple of minutes then turned and grabbed her. 'You hussy, c'm'ere.'

Clare went willingly, and that night they made love long and lingeringly, first on the rug in front of the fire, the flames casting dancing shadows over their naked bodies. Later, when the fire began to die down, Boyd lifted her in his arms and carried her up to their bedroom, laid her between the soft sheets and again kissed her into unbridled passion. They had made love so often during their marriage that it might easily have become like a pleasant habit by now, but every time was different, every time was new and exciting, lifting them both to the heights of joy. A wonderful shared experience that bound them more closely every time. Afterwards Boyd fell asleep, his arms still round her.

Clare lay with her head on his shoulder, feeling the rise and fall of his chest against her cheek. She felt satiated by love, all physical strength spent, but strangely she wasn't tired, not mentally anyway. Her thoughts went back over the evening and she smiled reminiscently as she remembered Boyd's triumphant excitement, but the smile faded as she thought of his plans for the future. He had wanted to please her, offering her a new car and suggesting a cottage in Provence. Both would be great fun—Clare was still young and worldly enough to be excited by them—but there had been no mention of children in his plans, and that saddened her. It was a subject on which it was becoming increasingly hard for her to talk to him. Impossible almost. It was as if he had now shut the idea of a family completely out of his mind. But whether Boyd was doing it because he didn't want to upset her or because he wasn't interested, Clare didn't know. On the few occasions when she'd tried to talk to him he'd merely said, very brusquely, 'That's over, Clare. Forget it,' and then changed the subject so that she couldn't pursue it.

She had tried to, of course; she wouldn't have been a female if she hadn't, but every time it had led to a row, ending with Clare getting over-emotional and bursting into tears, or Boyd turning on his heel and striding away. And each row had added another thickness to the barrier that Boyd had built round the subject, a barrier that he was much too resolute and clever to let her penetrate or undermine, however much he loved her. Feeling his arm protectively round her even in his sleep, and remembering the hours that they had just spent together, Clare was in no doubt that Boyd did love her, probably as much as he always had done. Perhaps even more. But did he really think he could cure this sadness in her heart by just ignoring it? Did he hope that time would dull her desire for motherhood until it just faded away? Sighing, Clare wriggled out of his embrace and moved over to her own side of the bed, trying to ignore the ache within her and finding no comfort from the man who should have been her strength and support.

During the next week Boyd was home late every night, working with the retiring sales director as they went over all the customer accounts and potential markets. To Boyd it was a courtesy thing, as he knew most of it anyway, and he could have picked up what he didn't know very easily. But the director wanted to do it, so there was no way Boyd was going to jeopardise his good will by refusing. And to Clare it was a relief because it gave her the chance to finish off the paintings she had been commissioned to do just within the deadline. She took the pictures up to the publisher's offices in London herself and came away glowing at their praise. That done, she stood on the pavement outside for a few moments, then took a deep breath—and plunged into shopping for a new outfit for the Christmas dinner and dance.

This year Clare felt almost as uptight as she had the first time; even if they wouldn't be sitting at the top table, everyone would know that Boyd had been promoted and would be sizing her up for director's wife potential. And Boyd had warned her that they would be expected to go and spend some time with the rest of the board and their wives so that they could be introduced to those they hadn't already met. There had been many social functions over the years, corporate entertainment mainly, that Clare had attended and where she had met other company wives, but even among the women—perhaps especially among the women—the hierarchy ladder had been maintained and she had tended to mix with the wives whose men were on the same rung of the ladder as Boyd. But Boyd had risen faster than anyone else, and now she would be expected to go up the social ladder with him. If not at his side, at least hanging on to his coat tails.

So now she would need a suitable dress. In the past she had managed to find good bargains at a dress-exchange shop run by a woman who had become a friend, but this time, urged on by Boyd, she spent a small fortune at an exclusive shop in Bond Street, the type that never displayed anything so common as the price on any of the gowns in their window. Clare took it home, thinking that it had cost almost as much as the commission she had earned on her paintings. But it was a beautiful dress, in a kind of coppery-gold material that changed colour as she moved and highlighted the chestnut glint in her hair. An unforgettable dress, and one that could be worn to the Christmas binge once in a lifetime. But there would probably be other times that she could wear it, and when she'd exhausted those she could always take it along to the exchange shop and sell it, Clare thought, easing the guilt.

There was the usual line of the president and the managing director and their wives, waiting to greet everyone as they arrived at the dinner. But this year Clare was greeted far more warmly than in the past, so warmly that they called her Clare and the managing director gave her a peck on the cheek. It was almost as if they were saying, 'Welcome aboard the board; you're one of us now.' She responded with a smile but wasn't sorry to move on to join a group of men and women from Boyd's sales team with their partners. But even here, where she'd been expecting to be able to relax among Boyd's friends, she sensed a subtle difference in their attitude towards her.

There was one man, Mike Carter, who had joined the company about the same time as Boyd, and they had risen up the ladder together for a few years, but now he was in charge of the market-research department and seemed likely to stay there. Clare looked on him, and his wife Sue, as friends, and said hello with real pleasure, but was taken aback by the stiff way they returned her greeting.

'What's the matter with Mike and Sue?' she asked Boyd at the first opportunity.

'He's sore because I got the directorship and he didn't.'

'Was he in line for it?'

'Not really. And what makes him even angrier is that he hasn't been offered my old job, either.'

'Who have they given it to?'

'Peter Stafford. He's only been with the company about three years.'

'Oh, yes, I know.' Clare wrinked her brow. 'He's what—about thirty-two? A couple of years younger than you?'

'Yes.'

'But Mike is older than you, isn't he?'

Boyd nodded. 'Exactly.'

'So this means that Mike is pretty much on the shelf?'

'I'm afraid so.'

'He seems to blame you for it. Did you have any say in who takes over your job?'

'Yes.' Boyd glanced at her, knowing what she was thinking. 'It's business, Clare; I'm not going to recommend someone I don't think is up to the job just because he's a friend.'

Clare gave a taut smile. '*Was* a friend.'

Boyd shrugged. 'Come on, let's mingle.'

Other people were more effusive—those who hadn't lost by Boyd's promotion and had everything to gain by being his friend. Clare received many flattering compliments on her appearance and was treated with a subtle deference that she hadn't expected and didn't want. When they were momentarily alone as people moved into couples to go into dinner she said in a low voice, 'I feel as if I'm in limbo.'

Boyd nodded in immediate understanding. 'I know what you mean.'

There were two empty spaces at their table in the dining-room and they weren't filled until halfway through the first course, when Peter Stafford and his wife hurried in, the woman red-faced, Peter clearly annoyed. As they sat down he said, 'Hello, everyone. I don't think you've met my wife Melanie.'

No one asked them for an explanation but his wife, a thin, harrassed-looking girl, said, 'So sorry we're late. The baby-sitter cancelled at the last minute and I had to go over and collect an aunt, but the traffic was bad and——'

'Could someone pass the wine?' her husband interrupted. 'I could do with a drink.'

His wife fell silent and Clare looked at her with sympathy, but perhaps that was a mistake because after dinner Melanie came to sit next to her and said, 'It's been a most terrible day. Everything seemed to go wrong. The childen always seem to know when we're going out and play up even more than they normally do. Don't you find that?'

'I haven't any children.'

Melanie gave her a surprised look, making Clare feel like some kind of freak. 'I haven't met you before, have I? This is the first time I've been to this dinner; last year the children were ill, and the year before that I was pregnant.'

'I'm Clare Russell.'

'Oh, Boyd's wife.'

'That's right. How many children have you got?'

'Three. We only intended to have two but the last pregnancy turned out to be twins.' Melanie leaned forward and said earnestly, 'Peter really admires Boyd. And we're so grateful that he helped him to get this new job. It's so expensive trying to bring up three children, you know, especially as Peter wants them to go to private schools.'

'Yes, I'm sure it must be.' Clare stood up, feeling that she shouldn't be hearing this. 'Excuse me. I must freshen up my lipstick.'

She made her way to the cloakroom and at the door met the managing director's wife again. 'A good dinner, I thought, didn't you?' the woman said as they went in.

'Delicious. Did you choose the menu?'

'Why, yes, that's part of *my* job,' the woman laughed. But then she said more seriously, 'I always think that, as well as supporting our husbands, we wives play a very important role when it comes to entertaining and events like this, don't you?'

'Oh, definitely,' Clare replied, because it was expected of her.

'And I'm sure you'll be a great asset to our "ladies' team", as I call it, my dear,' the older woman smiled. Adding, 'That dress is most becoming.'

'Thank you.' The director's wife went into a cubicle, while Clare went over to the mirrored wall and took out her lipstick. There was no one else there but a moment later the door swung open and Melanie came in. She came to sit on a stool beside Clare. 'They're all talking shop out there.' Melanie looked in the mirror and frowned, 'Lord, I know I look a mess, but I had to change in such a rush.' She began to comb her hair and said enviously, 'You look marvellous in that dress. I suppose you're used to this kind of thing. Peter says that we'll have to go to lots more functions now that he's been promoted.' She gave a worried sigh. 'I'm not sure that I want that. I never know what to say to people. Especially if they're older. I always feel a complete fool. I just know I'm going to let him down.'

'Nonsense, you'll get on fine,' Clare said bracingly, acutely conscious of the managing director's wife in the loo.

But Melanie went on, 'And it's going to be difficult to get baby-sitters to look after the kids all the time. Peter said that maybe we'll get a nanny, but I don't want to hand them over to someone just so that I can go and be pleasant to a lot of old fuddy-duddies and——'

'Shut up!' Clare whispered fiercely at her.

The other girl's mouth dropped open in startled amazement, but then the door of the cubicle opened and the other woman came out to wash her hands. Clare closed her evening bag and moved between the two, her back to Melanie. 'I thought your husband's speech was very witty,' she remarked. 'He must be used to being an after-dinner speaker.'

Behind her she heard the rustle of movement and knew that Melanie had wisely taken the opportunity to dash into a loo. Clare chatted with the director's wife and walked out of the cloakroom with her. The woman didn't say anything to Clare but she must have heard what Melanie had said, although with any luck she might be understanding enough not to say anything to her husband.

Back in the function-room a band had started to play, and Boyd swept her on to the floor to dance. 'You're the most beautiful woman here,' he told her.

'Watch it; flattery will get you anywhere.'

He grinned. 'I certainly hope so.'

As they danced Clare kept an eye on the cloakroom, but she didn't see Melanie come out. When the dance ended and they went back to their table Peter was still sitting with an empty chair beside him. He rose as they came up and said to Clare, 'Was Mellie OK?'

Clare sighed, not wanting to get involved, but said, 'I'll go and see, shall I?'

'If you wouldn't mind.' Peter gave her a charming smile. 'I'm afraid she might have a headache.'

Her biggest headache is probably you, Clare thought, wondering how the girl managed to cope with three children, two of them still babies, and a husband who obviously pressurised her.

Before going into the cloakroom Clare went to the bar and bought a large brandy, which she took in with her. Melanie was still locked in the loo. Clare waited until the cloakroom was empty and then banged on the door and called, 'Melanie, it's Clare. You can't stay in there all night, so you might as well come out.'

'I can't.' The words came out on a sob.

'If you stay in there any longer people will think you're ill and they'll send someone to break the door down. Peter wouldn't like that.'

This threat brought Melanie out, her face streaked with tears. Clare pushed her down on to a seat and said, 'Here, drink this. And don't say you don't like it—it's medicinal.'

Obediently Melanie drank it, pulling a face as she did so. 'Ugh.'

'Now, where's your make-up? You must repair your face or everyone will know you've been crying.'

'What's the use,' Melanie said with a groan. 'That woman is bound to tell her husband.'

'Not necessarily. Anyway, she probably feels the same way herself.'

Melanie didn't look as if she believed her. 'Peter will kill me. He said I had to make a good impression to-night.' Bitterly she added, 'And I thought you came to this kind of thing to have a good time.'

'You've got a lot to learn,' Clare told her. 'The company might give out the official message to relax and enjoy yourself, but the unspoken message is: don't relax too much, don't drink too much, don't say or do anything that may offend anybody. You shouldn't have spoken to me as you did, for a start; I might have reported back.'

Melanie looked at her in horror. 'But you're so nice. I thought—I thought...'

'No, you didn't think first, Melanie. But you're going to have to watch yourself all the time if you want to help your husband.'

The warning didn't make the other girl any happier. 'Sometimes I wonder if it's all worth it,' she said miserably.

'Of course it is; you have your children to consider. Now come on, put on your make-up or else Peter will be sending out another search party.'

'I can't face him. He'll kill me when I tell him.'

'So don't tell him. Why spoil his evening and both be miserable?'

'But he'll want to know why I've been in here so long.'

'Well, we'll say that someone stepped on the hem of your dress and tore it and you've had to sew it up.'

Melanie gave a sudden laugh. 'I was right to like you.'

'That's better. Ready?' Clare smiled at her encouragingly.

'I suppose so.'

Peter was sitting with Boyd but was keeping a sharp eye out for Melanie and got to his feet as they came up. Clare smiled at him. 'You'll have to buy Melanie a little sewing kit for Christmas; someone trod on her skirt and tore the hem. Luckily I was able to come to her rescue.'

Peter's face flooded with relief, but Clare turned away to drop her evening bag on the table, then say to Boyd, 'Come on, let's dance.'

It was a slow number, which was nice because Boyd could hold her in his arms. 'I didn't know you carried a sewing kit around with you.'

'Of course. I was a Brownie—always prepared.'

'Those were the Scouts.'

She made a face at him. 'Don't be pedantic.'

Boyd glanced across at where Peter and Melanie were dancing, the girl talking too much. 'What was really wrong with Melanie?'

Usually Clare had no secrets from Boyd, but she decided that it would be betraying Melanie's confidence to tell him, so she merely said, 'A female problem.'

Boyd gave her an exasperated look. 'What's that supposed to mean?' He looked across at Melanie again. 'I haven't met her before. I hope she isn't going to let him down. A man needs a wife who's an asset in this game.'

'It shouldn't matter a damn what his wife is like,' Clare said hotly. 'He should be judged on his own efforts, not on whether his wife is suitable and sufficiently supportive.'

'He was, but the wives play an important role when it comes to public relations, you know that,' Boyd said mildly.

'In that case, they should be paid for the hours they spend in helping to promote the company,' she said forcefully. 'You can put *that* idea to the board when you attend your first directors' meeting.'

Boyd grinned. 'I can just imagine their faces.'

'And I can imagine exactly what their reply would be: we give the ladies all these wonderful treats; days at the races, Wimbledon, the Chelsea Flower Show—and they want *paying* for it!'

'Well, they have a point.' But Boyd laughed, then nodded to Peter and Melanie as they danced past them. 'She doesn't look very happy. What was really wrong with her?' he asked again.

'Oh, nothing—just that being a wife, mother, housekeeper, chauffeur, cleaner, laundress, and now having to be her husband's accessory at this social minefield got the better of her for a few minutes.'

Boyd's eyebrows rose at her tone. 'Lucky you, then, to be just an artist, a wife, and my most dazzling adornment.' And he learned forward to lightly kiss her lips.

Clare might have made some retort to that description, but a voice said jovially, 'Put that woman down, Boyd. Can't you wait till you get home?'

They turned and saw John Broome, the sales director, the man whose job Boyd was taking over, and his wife dancing along beside them. So they all stopped so that they could exchange greetings, the women kissing each other like old friends and being kissed by the other's husband. They talked for a little, then John said with a wink, 'How about swapping wives, Boyd?'

Boyd laughed dutifully and passed Clare over.

'How do you intend to pass your time when you retire?' she asked as she began to dance with the older man.

'Oh, play a lot of golf, I expect. Catch up on all the odd jobs, that kind of thing.'

There was something in his voice that made Clare look at him more closely. He wasn't a tall man but he was hefty and big-boned, the jovial sort who didn't mind making people laugh even at his own expense, everyone's friend, especially when it came to customers. But

Clare noticed that he had lost a lot of weight, that his skin sagged and had an unhealthy grey pallor. His good-humour, too, seemed forced. She didn't know his age but as he was retiring he must be sixty, she supposed. Looking at him, Clare realised now that his fullness of face and air of conviviality had made him appear much younger than he actually was.

'I expect you'll be taking holidays, too, won't you?' she ventured.

'Holidays?' His voice became suddenly bitter. 'Retirement is supposed to be one long holiday, isn't it?'

'It is if you're young enough to enjoy it, I suppose,' Clare said cautiously.

'Yes, I suppose a couple of weeks here and there relieve the boredom while you sit around and wait to die.'

Clare stared at him, feeling suddenly apprehensive. 'Don't you want to retire, John?'

'I don't have any choice. Didn't Boyd tell you? I have this bloody ulcer that won't clear up. They say it's due to stress. That if I don't pack up work I'll probably have a coronary.' He looked down at her. 'How old do you think I am?' Clare shook her head wordlessly, afraid to make a guess. 'Forty-nine, that's all. I could have gone on for another ten years.' His grip on her hand suddenly tightened. 'Boyd's ambitious,' he said shortly. 'Don't let him overdo it or he'll end up like me.'

'No, all right,' she said faintly.

The music came to an end and she couldn't help being glad. It had been a shock to see the real man under the jovial mask, and terrible to know that he was ill.

When she went back to Boyd she was a little subdued, but he hardly noticed; too many people were congratulating him on his promotion and he was on a high. It wasn't until the evening was over and they were back in the car, driving home, that he became aware of her absorption. 'Tired?' he asked.

'No, not really.'

'Did you enjoy the evening?'

'It was OK.'

Boyd grimaced. 'That sounds as if you didn't. Anything specific, or did you find the whole thing boring?' he asked, his tone cool.

After hesitating a moment, Clare said, 'Are you sure about this new job, Boyd?'

'Sure about it?' He took his eyes off the road for a moment to give her an astonished glance. 'Of course I'm sure. What do you think I've been working for during these last eight years? Did someone say that I wasn't right for the job? Is that it?'

'No, of course not. And I know you've worked hard, terribly hard.'

'What's this all about, then?'

Slowly Clare answered, 'I'm beginning to wonder if the job is right for you, for anyone, really.'

'Someone has to do it,' Boyd said impatiently. 'And whoever does it gets the rewards.'

'Yes,' Clare agreed drily. 'But they may get more than they bargained for.'

Pulling into the side of the road, Boyd stopped the car and turned to look at her. 'Just what is this all about, Clare?'

'You didn't tell me that John Broome was retiring because of illness. You let me think he'd reached retirement age.'

'I don't remember saying anything either way.' He shrugged. 'What does it matter, anyway? He's retiring and that's all there is to it.'

'It isn't that simple,' Clare said hotly. 'John says he has an ulcer and that it was caused by stress. Stress brought on by his job. And you're taking over that job. Don't you think I have the right to be worried?'

'It isn't the job,' Boyd answered tersely. 'It's his way of life. He drinks too much, has too many meals with clients, and doesn't get any exercise. Anyone who lives like that is asking for trouble.'

'He plays golf—that's exercise.' Immediately she'd said it Clare regretted it, realising that she was already on the defensive. 'But he's only forty-nine and he looks sixty. I don't want you to end up like that in another twenty years or even less.'

'I won't; I'm far more active than he is.'

'Yes—now. But how many hundreds of business lunches and dinners are you going to have to get through before——?'

'Look, Clare, just leave it, will you? John was a fool to have said anything to you. He's just fed up that he's having to give it all up. He knows I won't allow him to take it out on me, so he started on you. Forget him, he isn't important.' And he cursed under his breath.

But she immediately said, 'I think you're wrong. OK, he's bitter at being ill, but I think he genuinely wanted to warn us.' Boyd made a disbelieving sound, but she went on, 'I know you want this job, that it's been your big ambition since you joined the firm, but maybe your obsession with it has clouded your vision. Have you ever stopped to look at what the job entails—the hours, the travelling?'

'It's nothing I can't handle,' he said shortly. 'Look, let's drop this; I want to get home.'

'No.' She reached out and put a restraining hand on his arm when he went to start the car. 'I'm used to that tactic; you'll keep finding excuses to put off talking about it until I get fed up and drop it. I want to talk about it now.'

'There's nothing to talk about. I've been offered the job and I've accepted it; end of story.'

'And did it occur to you to ask me what I thought?'

'No, because you were right behind me until you had this stupid talk with John Broome. I've told you I can do it. Don't worry about it.'

'But you'll be away from home more. We'll be apart more.'

He shrugged, unable to deny it. 'Possibly.'

'Maybe I don't want that.'

'We'll have a much better quality of life when we are together,' he pointed out.

'But maybe I'd rather have the kind of life we have now and see you more often. Perhaps it might even be possible for you to get a job where you didn't have to go away at all.'

Boyd turned again to face her, his tone angry now as he said, 'Just what are you trying to say, Clare?'

She knew that she was beating her head against a brick wall, but went on stubbornly, 'Why do we need all this extra money, anyway? We hardly have enough time together to spend what you make now. If you got an easier job and I worked as well then we could see much more of each other. After all, we—we have no one else we need to spend money on or save for. There's only the two of us.'

'I wondered when you'd get around to that,' Boyd said acidly.

Clare bit her lip. 'It's still a fact.'

'One you keep forcing down my throat.' Boyd lifted a hand to push his hair off his forehead, then sighed heavily. 'I'm sorry. But you knew when you married me that I was determined to get on. OK, maybe I will be away more at first but I promise to try to keep it to the minimum. And I won't push myself too far. I'll delegate as much as I possibly can and I'll take you with me whenever I can. It will be fun going places together.'

But Clare had been away on business trips with Boyd a few times before and knew that he seldom saw much of the places apart from his hotel and the conference centre. Sometime the conference was even held in the same hotel so he saw nothing of the country. And she had been left alone all day, often far into the evening, to amuse herself. The thought of years of such travel appalled her. 'I don't want that. You know what I want.'

Reaching across, Boyd took her hand. 'I know it's hard, but please try and accept it, my darling. We have each other.'

'I want to hold a child of my own in my arms,' she said brokenly.

Boyd took her in *his* arms. 'I know, but it just isn't to be.' He kissed her forehead and said, 'You're all I want, my love, all I've ever wanted. So long as I have you I shall always be happy.'

She pushed him away angrily. 'You don't understand what it's like for a woman to want a child; it isn't the same for you.'

'No, I don't understand,' Boyd said, his voice hardening. 'Aren't I enough for you, then?'

Clare lifted her head to look at him, then said emphatically, 'No. No, you're not.'

CHAPTER THREE

USUALLY, when they'd had a quarrel, they made it up in bed, but when Clare and Boyd got home that night the row was so recent that they were still angry with each other. When they got into bed Boyd merely said, 'Goodnight,' shortly and turned away from her to go to sleep almost at once. Clare lay awake for a little longer, angry with the company, Boyd, and herself, in that order, and thinking what a waste of time the whole evening had been. But Boyd had enjoyed it—apart from the inquest on the way home, of course, but then, it was his world, a world that Clare found was becoming increasingly distant from her own. She sighed, her thoughts unhappy as she fell asleep.

It seemed that they weren't the only couple to have had a row on the way home from the dinner dance. When Boyd went off to play squash the next morning Clare took the opportunity to phone Melanie Stafford. She hesitated quite a bit before doing so, not wanting to be involved but feeling a sense of responsibility and finally dialling the number. Luckily it was Melanie who answered.

'Hello, it's Clare Russell. We met last night at the——'

'Oh, yes, of course. Hello. How are you?'

'I'm fine. Is—er—everything OK?' Clare asked cautiously, aware that Melanie's husband might be within earshot.

'It's all right, Peter's playing rugby,' Melanie said baldly. Then she sighed. 'I didn't tell Peter what happened in the cloakroom, but he had a go at me on the way home; he said I had too much to drink and I was unsociable.'

'What did he mean by that?'

'That I didn't make a point of being pleasant to the directors, I suppose. But I just couldn't after what that woman had heard me say; suppose she'd already told them all? I'd have died.'

'You did the right thing,' Clare assured her. 'It will all be forgotten by next time.'

Melanie groaned. 'I'd give anything for there not to be a next time. I'm going to kill Peter's career, I just know it.'

'No, you won't, you'll soon get used to it.'

'Clare?' Melanie hesitated, but Clare knew by the way the other girl had said her name that she was going to ask a favour. 'You're so experienced at this kind of thing, so sophisticated—do you think we could get together and have a talk? I really need some help.'

Clare agreed with the latter remark, but said, 'I'm not really the one to advise you, Melanie. I'm too anti. You want to talk to someone who enjoys being a company wife, who's enthusiastic about it. Don't you have any friends who can help you?'

'No, we've just moved to a bigger house on this new estate and I hardly know anyone here.'

'How about your mother? Or some other member of your family?'

'No, there's no one who has this kind of experience. Please, Clare, couldn't you come over here one afternoon and——?'

Clare thought of Melanie's babies and said abruptly, 'No. Sorry.'

For a moment Melanie was taken aback by her rudeness, then said in a stiff, hollow voice, 'Of course not. I quite understand. I'm sorry I asked. Well, thanks for phoning. Goodbye.'

'Wait!' Melanie's tone made her feel rotten, so, against her better judgement, Clare said, 'I didn't mean I wouldn't try to help you. I just think it would be better if we met for lunch or something. Just the two of us, without the children. So that you can concentrate.'

'Oh, I see. Yes, OK. I'll have to arrange a baby-sitter, though. When can you make it?'

'Let's leave it until after Christmas and the New Year, shall we? There's plenty of time before the next company function. How about if I give you a ring sometime towards the end of January?'

'Yes, fine.' But Melanie must have thought it was just a polite put-off, because the disappointment was still in her voice.

'I *will* phone,' Clare assured her before saying goodbye.

She put the receiver down, wishing that she'd never picked it up. She didn't want to get drawn into Melanie's problems, and she certainly didn't want to go to her home and see her children, the children that Clare so much envied.

For a few moments Clare stood clenching her fists, trying to control her feelings, then pulled on a pair of rubber gloves and spent an energetic couple of hours doing all the rotten jobs around the house, like cleaning the cooker and the freezer, the sort of chores she always left until she couldn't escape them any longer. When Boyd came home only her lower half was visible as she stretched to reach the bottom of the chest freezer. Patting her familiarly on the behind, he said, 'You do realise it's Sunday, don't you?'

Clare straightened up and said, 'I know we agreed I wouldn't do any housework on Sundays, but I felt like it.' And she faced him defiantly.

'Do whatever you want, my darling,' Boyd said soothingly. 'It's just that it's almost one o'clock and there doesn't seem to be any lunch cooking.'

Clare laughed. 'And I thought you were thinking of me!' She put her hands on her hips. 'I suppose you're starving?'

Putting his arms round her waist, Boyd pulled her to him and began to nibble her ear. 'I shall have to eat you unless you produce something fast.'

'Well, you have a choice: me or lunch at the pub.'

'How about both?' Boyd said thickly, kissing his way down her throat.

'Oh, no!' She pushed him away. 'Help me put this food back in the freezer and then we'll walk up to the pub.'

He obeyed her in mock meekness but got both the things he wanted anyway, because they had a bottle of wine with their lunch which made them feel mellow and sexy, so that they spent the rest of the afternoon in bed.

'You always get turned on when you drink wine,' Boyd said in pleased satisfaction at one point.

'That's right,' Clare agreed sleepily. 'Three glasses of wine and I'm anybody's.'

'You mean mine.' Boyd ran an appreciative hand along the curve of her hip.

'Oh, no—you're just the one who happens to be around all the time,' she mocked.

'You she-devil! I'll show you that you don't need anyone else.' Which he did, very satisfactorily.

They slept for a while, then went downstairs and re-lit the fire in the sitting-room. 'We've got to work out our Christmas present list,' Clare said determinedly, fetching a notepad. 'We just can't leave it any longer.'

It was something she said every year and, as usual, a hunted look immediately came into Boyd's eyes. 'Why don't I go and phone Mother and ask if there's anything special she or Dad would like?' he offered, as he always did.

Wryly Clare watched him pick up the phone, knowing that his mother would say, as she did every year, 'Clare buys such clever presents; we'd much rather leave it to her.' Then Boyd would chat to his parents for another half an hour and then duck out, considering that to be his contribution to Christmas.

Clare didn't enjoy Christmas any more. They always divided the holiday into spending Boxing Day at Boyd's grandmother's home with all his family, and Christmas Day with her family, but Clare's mother, a widow, lived so far away that she always insisted they go on Christmas Eve, so it usually worked out that they had no time at all in their own home. But even so it meant a lot of work for Clare because she had to buy the presents for both families and, as she was an artist and therefore creative, she was expected to produce unusual, clever gifts that were always beautifully wrapped. That it was partly her own fault, Clare knew; the first two or three Christmases she had known Boyd she had naturally wanted to please and impress his parents and family and so had taken a great deal of trouble over their gifts, and she had created a standard that it was hard work to keep up, especially when she was living in the country, where shopping was more difficult and limited.

Although Boyd was an only child, his father came from a large family, which gathered, every Boxing Day, at his grandmother's house. Sometimes there were as many as forty people there, especially now that some of

Boyd's cousins, his contemporaries, were having children of their own. It hurt Clare to see the young mothers with their babies, and it didn't help that they all knew about her miscarriages, about the doctor saying that she would be unlikely ever to carry a child full term. Sometimes, in misguided kindness, someone would offer her a baby to hold, but doing so tore at Clare's heart, and she couldn't wait to leave, coming away from the party feeling thoroughly dejected.

On Monday morning she again had to leave her painting and go up to London with Boyd, to push her way through the crowds of shoppers, her Christmas present list clasped in her hand, but forever changing it as the things she wanted were unavailable or she saw something she liked better. It cost a fortune, too, money that would probably be wasted if the boxes of unwanted gifts she and Boyd had stashed away in the loft were anything to go by. Next year I'm going to boycott Christmas, she thought indignantly as another harassed middle-aged shopper trod heavily on her foot. I'm not going to buy a single present and I'm going to insist that we spend the holiday at home, just the two of us. But she had been thinking the same rebellious thoughts for the last few years and still hadn't found the courage to carry them out. The emotional blackmail from both families had been too strong. They were expected; it would be breaking with tradition: everyone would be so upset if they didn't go. Clare's tentative attempts to break away had been met with plaintive protests, especially from her own mother, who had the more excuse as she had only Clare and Clare's brother and his family to visit her.

When Clare met Boyd at the office that evening she was tired, footsore, and dejected. Slumping down into a chair, she kicked off her shoes and said, 'Give me a drink before I pass out.'

'Here.' Boyd thrust a fast gin and tonic in her hand. 'Bad, was it?'

'Terrible. I will never, ever do this again,' she swore in fervent tones.

'You say that every year. Why don't you stagger buying the presents through the year instead of leaving it until the last minute?'

'And you say that every year. You know full well why; because I'm so glad to get Christmas over that I don't want to think about it again until I absolutely have to.' She took a long swallow of the drink. 'Oh, that is delicious.' Boyd was sitting on the edge of his desk, watching her, his mouth curled in amusement. 'Why can't we go away to a hotel somewhere for Christmas? Just the two of us?'

'I don't want to go to an impersonal hotel.'

'All right, we'll just tell people we're going to a hotel, but we'll stay at home and hide. Take the phone off the hook and not see anyone else for a whole week. We'll have our own Christmas tree, and our own dinner, which we'll eat when we like, and we'll leave the washing-up until we feel like doing it. We could open our presents in bed and not get up until we want to. Heaven! Bliss!' She gave him a pleading look. 'Let's do it, Boyd.'

'And let the parents down?'

'Your family is so large that we wouldn't be missed, and my mother would have two people less to fuss herself silly over. I think it's a great idea.'

'You're not serious?'

'Yes, I am. Wouldn't you like to spend Christmas by ourselves?'

'We're by ourselves the rest of the year; don't you think it rather selfish not to visit our families when they most want to see us?'

He spoke reasonably, as if she were a rather silly, rebellious child, and for a brief moment she felt a flash of emotion that was close to hatred. That she could feel such a thing for Boyd temporarily horrified her, but she got abruptly to her feet, and said caustically, 'It's all right for you, you don't have to shop or wrap presents. And when it comes to Christmas all you and the other men do is sit around, drinking and talking, while the women cook and serve and clear up, and talk about their children all the time!'

Boyd frowned and straightened up. 'Is that what this is all about?' Coming over to her, he put his hands on her shoulders. 'You've got to learn to live with it, darling.'

She lifted pain-racked green eyes to meet his. 'Do we have to go?'

'It's too late to back out this year, but next Christmas I promise to take you away somewhere.' She gave a sigh, latching on to a promise even that distant as a non-swimmer did to a lifebelt. Boyd began to stroke her hair. 'You're worn out. Why don't you have a rest here on the couch for an hour before you change?'

They were taking John Broome and his wife out to dinner that evening as a thank-you for his recommending Boyd to take over his job. Clare had brought a dress up to London with her that morning, intending to change in Boyd's office. 'Maybe I will. The shops were so crowded,' she said by way of excuse, but they both knew that the three miscarriages in a row had sapped her strength and vitality.

'Finish your drink.'

Clare did so, and Boyd led her over to the couch, found a cushion to lean her head on and gently rubbed her poor feet. She closed her eyes with a sigh. 'That feels *so* good.' Boyd went on stroking her until he was sure that she was asleep, then looked at her for a long moment before going back to his desk to continue working.

It was over an hour later when he kissed her awake. Still half asleep, Clare put her arms round his neck to return his kiss, her mouth opening languorously under his, expecting the kiss to lead to sex, as it so often did when he kissed her awake. Boyd chuckled softly against her mouth. 'Not right now, my darling.'

'Why not?' she murmured, then became aware that she was dressed and not in bed. Opening her eyes, she saw where she was and remembered why. 'What's the time?'

'Six forty-five.'

'I'd better change, then.'

She carried her dress along to the ladies' cloakroom further down the corridor. The place was empty, most of the staff long gone home. The rest had done her good, and the familiar task of washing, changing and making-up again put Clare in a much better frame of mind, so that she had a big smile for Boyd when she went back to his office.

'That's my girl.' He kissed her neck, glad that she was all right again, and helped her on with her coat. 'Let's go.'

'But we have to put all the shopping in the car.' She looked round, but the pile of plastic carriers was gone.

'All done. All we have to do is go.'

The Broomes soon joined them, John's wife having travelled up to town by train, and they walked to the restaurant. Somewhat to her own surprise, Clare enjoyed the evening. She had been rather apprehensive after

John's outburst at the dinner dance, but if he felt any bitterness tonight he kept it well hidden. He was his usual outwardly ebullient self. For his wife's sake, Clare thought, watching him. He wants her to have a good time. In fact, both men put themselves out to please their wives, hardly mentioning work, and Boyd carefully avoided the subject of Christmas, steering the conversation away when it got close. It was an expensive restaurant but the food and the service were worth it.

'I enjoyed tonight,' Clare said when they got back to the car and began the drive home.

'Good.' Boyd smiled at her, obviously pleased. 'We must go there again.' Reaching out, he squeezed her knee, an affectionate gesture he often used. But not so much lately, Clare realised.

'Am I getting grouchy?' she asked with sudden insight.

Boyd laughed. 'You have your moments. But I'm sure I do as well.'

'Yes, you do,' Clare agreed, so feelingly that they both laughed this time.

'But at least we don't get grouchy in bed,' Boyd remarked with a grin.

Clare remembered the way he had turned his back on her after the row they'd had over the dinner dance, but Boyd had obviously forgotten, so she just smiled back and said, 'No, never that.'

The whole of the next day Clare spent writing out Christmas cards, another job that had somehow always been left to her. It was a chore she didn't object to too much, as it brought to mind friends they hadn't seen for a while, to whom she enclosed a letter of news. But Boyd had given her a list of people he wanted cards sent to, business friends and colleagues in the company mostly, a list that grew longer every year and which threatened to get out of hand this Christmas. 'Why can't you get

Velma the Vamp to send them?' Clare said in dismay
when she looked at the list he gave her that morning just
before we went to work.

'She already sends the official company cards; these
are personal ones.' Boyd gave her a persuasive kiss on
the neck. 'Buy you a box of your favourite chocolates,'
he bribed.

'A box! This lot will cost you at least three. And you
can stick your own stamps on,' she yelled after him as
he went out of the door.

Writing the cards and letters took her nearly all day,
but at length she sat back with a sigh and regarded the
piles of envelopes with some satisfaction. There were well
over a hundred cards, and she'd used almost all that
she'd bought. Clare went to put away the odd ones that
were left, but on top of the pile there was the copy of
a painting of an eastern-looking city in winter. It made
Clare think of Warsaw and the Prizbilskis, and on im-
pulse she wrote a card to them, too. Her back ached
from sitting down for so long. Getting to her feet, Clare
stretched, made herself a coffee, then wandered round
the house as she drank it. Almost automatically her steps
took her into her studio, the walls painted white to re-
flect the light that came in through the big windows.

Her work was as she had left it, days before, a picture
of an exotic island with palm-trees and a galleon moored
in the lagoon for a book jacket. Thinking that she would
work for just half an hour, Clare sat down at her work-
bench and soon became immersed in her painting, fascinated and completely absorbed by it, so that she forgot
the time, forgot everything else. She came to with a start
when she heard Boyd's car drive up to the house, but
he was good about her not having prepared any dinner
and went out again to get Chinese, and she made a special
effort to listen with interest when he talked about the

trade fair he was helping to organise for the following year.

'You must go with me to that,' he said firmly. 'It's in Bruges, which I'm told is a beautiful city.'

Recognising his tone, Clare said, 'Yes, OK,' knowing that even if she objected she wouldn't win.

There were other duty functions to go to before Christmas: the members of the board had their own party, to which she and Boyd were invited for the first time. Not a very relaxed evening for either of them, but some of the women were nice and it went off OK. They also had to attend another dinner given for the firm's customers, an important occasion for Boyd, this, and one at which Clare was expected to be especially charming to everyone, but where she was in constant dread of not remembering names and faces from last year. Then there was the nicer side of Christmas, when they went to drinks parties with friends and neighbours, where they could really relax and enjoy themselves. Clare loved those. But then Peter and Melanie Stafford invited them out to dinner to say thank-you in their turn for Boyd's recommending Peter for promotion.

They met up at a restaurant in town that Clare knew was terribly expensive and which she worried Peter could ill afford with three young children to provide for. Melanie was wearing a new bright blue dress that was too harsh for her pale colouring, and she was withdrawn at first. But after a couple of glasses of wine she changed completely and chattered away like the friendly, trusting girl she was. Or at least she did until her husband must have kicked her under the table, and Melanie stopped abruptly, her cheeks flushing bright red. At the time she had started to tell them how much she hated it when Peter had to go away and she was left alone in the house, so maybe he had cause, but Clare thought it was a shame that the other girl had to watch what she said all the time.

Clare said as much to Boyd on the way home. 'Peter is going to kill all Melanie's spontaneity if he isn't careful.'

'She's too naïve; she should watch herself more,' Boyd rejoined.

'Surely her naturalness is the most attractive thing about her.'

He was silent a moment, considering it, then nodded. 'You may be right, but what was OK in a girlfriend won't do for the wife of an upwardly mobile executive.'

'So Peter has to kill what probably drew him to her in the first place.' Clare gave a rather harsh laugh. 'And Melanie has to subjugate her natural personality to become a company wife, if she wants to keep her marriage going.'

'If she loves him she'll do it.'

'If he loved her he wouldn't make her do it,' Clare retorted, her voice becoming angry. 'He would allow her—want her—to be herself.'

Boyd put his hand on her knee. 'It isn't our business,' he said soothingly. 'They must sort it out for themselves.'

Clare hesitated, then said, 'Melanie has asked me to help her. She wants me to teach her how a company wife should behave. Me! That's pretty ironic, don't you think?'

Boyd cursed under his breath. 'She had no right to ask you.'

'Why not? Who else should she ask? Someone has to take the poor girl under her wing and teach her how to go on.'

'No one taught you. You've always been great at that kind of thing.'

'Just a natural creep,' Clare said on a note of self-contempt.

'Don't be ridiculous. All that's needed is to be polite, pleasant, and reasonably intelligent. But in your case you shone because you're more than intelligent: you're interested in people, have great vitality, and share my ambitions. Or at least you used to,' he added after a moment.

Her voice husky, Clare put a grateful hand on his arm. 'Thanks.'

'But I'm right, aren't I? You no longer share my ambitions.'

After hesitating for a moment, Clare nodded and admitted, 'I guess my hopes for the future changed direction somewhere along the line.'

'But does that mean that you can't still share mine?'

'Oh, but I do,' she protested. 'I'm still pleased that you've got what you wanted. But you would have got there without me.'

'Nonsense!' Boyd's voice was firm, certain. 'I've always needed your help—and I need it now. Without you beside me there's no point to any of this.'

Clare wasn't sure that she believed him, wasn't sure that he really believed it himself, but she was grateful and leaned over to kiss him on the cheek.

Boyd grinned widely. 'Hey, don't interfere with the driver!'

And so what could have developed into another row was diverted. Why do we always seem to argue in the car nowadays? Clare thought. Probably because it was the only place, except bed, where they were alone without anything else to distract them. But thinking of the car led her on to a safe subject. 'Have you decided what make your new company car will be yet?'

With Boyd's promotion had come a higher status car of his own choice, and he had spent several happily engrossed hours poring over car brochures and magazines. 'I think I'll have a Merc,' he said now. 'Something that will eat up the miles when I have to go to Europe.'

'Sounds great. What colour?'

'What colour would you like? You choose.'

'How about silver?' They talked cars for a while and then fell silent, Clare leaning back against the head-rest. Her thoughts went back to Melanie and how she would have to change if she wanted to be a good company wife. She wondered if she herself had changed much to fit the image. She couldn't remember having done so, but perhaps it had happened so gradually that she hadn't realised. Or had Boyd married her precisely because she already had all the attributes he needed to help him in his chosen career? That thought brought a nasty taste to Clare's mouth. She fervently hoped that they had married for more than that. She certainly had. She had fallen headlong in love with Boyd almost as soon as she had started dating him, and it wouldn't have mattered whether he was ambitious or not, she would still have married him.

Or would she? The thought came unbidden into her mind. Hadn't she, too, been ambitious for all the material things of their world? Would she have loved him so readily if he'd been placid and unconcerned for the future? Wryly Clare thought that she, like all women before her, right back to the Stone Age, had looked for a suitable mate, one to give her a comfortable home and security, to provide for her and her children. So much for equality of the sexes. And Boyd had given her all that she wanted and more. He had even given her the children; it wasn't his fault that she'd been unable to keep them. It wasn't his fault, either, that her hopes had changed. She didn't want just to be the wife of a successful man any more, she wanted to be a mother as well. Tears came to Clare's eyes and she blinked them away as she thought that her hopes seemed unlikely ever to be fulfilled. And going to parties, having to smile and look happy all the time was very hard when all she wanted was just to shut herself away and grieve for her three lost babies. To lose herself in her painting, which was the only therapy that helped her to forget.

People expected her to be over it by now, both physically and mentally—after all, it was nearly six months since the last miscarriage—but sometimes Clare felt so low, so dejected, that she could do nothing but cry. Mostly she managed to hide these bouts of depression from Boyd, and her doctor had given her some pills that helped, but sometimes the ache of grief was like a physical pain in her heart that she had to fight to conquer.

The nicest thing about Christmas, Clare thought one morning as she picked up the post from the mat, was receiving greetings cards in return. It was very close to Christmas, and there was a pile of cards today. Clare took them into the kitchen to open over a cup of coffee. Boyd had gone to work and wouldn't be home till around seven, so she had the whole day to herself, although a great deal of it would have to be spent on wrapping parcels. There were cards from old art-college friends, some of them painted by themselves, often comic, which made her laugh and think nostalgically of the past. And there were the more formal ones with printed names inside from Boyd's business colleagues and the company directors. There were several, too, with foreign stamps, from friends who had gone to live abroad or from people Boyd had become friendly with on his continental business trips. And there was one with a Polish stamp, from Mr and Mrs Prizbilski.

Clare opened the card and read the greeting, and was mildly surprised to find that there was also a long letter of several pages inside the envelope. She poured herself another coffee and settled down to read it, finding it rather difficult as Mrs Prizbilski's written English wasn't as good as her spoken. Slowly Clare deciphered the letter, reading the expected thanks for their hospitality and how all Mrs Prizbilski's family and friends had liked the gifts that Clare had helped to choose for them. Then the tone of the letter changed as the Polish woman went into a long story about some young neighbours of hers who had been killed in a car crash recently. Mrs Prizbilski wrote:

> They had two children. They are a pair. One girl. One boy. And their age is only six months. At now the teenaged sister of the wife takes care of them. There is no one else in family. But soon the sister will go to Warsaw, to university. She cannot take the babies there, so they must be with another family.

At this point there were several words crossed out, as if the writer had looked for the word she wanted but been unable to find it. The letter went on,

> But no one wants two children who are a pair. So they must go to an orphanage and perhaps someone will take one, someone else another. But I think that perhaps you and Boyd would like to be the new mother and father for these children. It could be done. The sister is willing. And there is no one else who can take them. No grandmothers or grandfathers. What do you think? They are pretty children with light hair, and their mother and father were good people and clever. Will you help them? Will you take them for your own?

Clare put the letter down abruptly and got agitatedly to her feet. Her heart was full of sympathy for the two children, twins, she supposed, but how could Mrs Prizbilski possibly suggest that they adopt them? It was unthinkable. Adoption had been mentioned to her before, by the doctor at the hospital, and by other well-meaning people, but to Clare it underlined her own sense of failure. She wanted her own child, hers and Boyd's, a boy who would look like him, or a girl whom she could teach to paint. And she hadn't yet given up hope of that; she still clung to her dream, hoping that medical science would help her, that if she tried again . . . But the doctors had offered no hope, and Boyd had made her promise not to. For her own sake, because she was wearing herself out physically and got so depressed when things went wrong yet again. So adoption, as far as Clare was concerned, was a no-go word. Without bothering to read the rest of the letter, she thrust it back into its envelope and threw it into the waste-bin, her hands shaking.

She ran into the sitting-room, pulled out rolls of pretty seasonal paper from the cupboards and began to attack the pile of presents waiting to be wrapped as if they were an enemy army that had to be overcome. The radio she put on good and loud, too, but nothing could shut out the picture of those two poor orphaned babies. Anger filled Clare's heart. How could Mrs Prizbilski even suggest such a thing? There must be thousands of couples in Poland who would want to adopt them. And, surely, it was wrong for them to leave their own country? The whole idea was absolutely ridiculous. Ludicrous. But still Clare couldn't put them out of her mind, so in the end she just abandoned the parcels and went into her studio to seek the solace of painting.

She had set the alarm clock for five, so that she wouldn't forget the time again. After cleaning her brushes, Clare went into the kitchen to prepare the evening meal, and when the casserole was in the oven collected up the rubbish and went to throw it into the bin. There, almost as if it was reproaching her, lay the crumpled letter from Mrs Prizbilski. She stood and stared at it for a long moment, then reached in and retrieved it before throwing the rubbish away. Perhaps she had made a mistake. Perhaps the Polish woman's English was so bad that Clare had misread the letter.

She hadn't, of course. The two babies were still being cared for by a teenaged girl who didn't want them, who— naturally enough—wanted to get on with her own life, find her own husband and have her own children. But it was still nothing to do with her! Clare shoved the letter out of sight again, but in a drawer in the bureau this time. But it wasn't so easy to forget, especially as there was the problem of answering it. She didn't have to, of course; she hadn't asked Mrs Prizbilski to interfere in her life and she could just ignore the letter. But the Polish woman had been nice and had obviously made the suggestion in the kindest way, so to ignore it would be rude. And, besides, she might think that Clare hadn't got the letter and would write again. So a brief, firm note saying that she had no interest whatsoever in adoption was all that was needed. But she wouldn't do it now, not today. There was plenty of time.

Boyd came home and, after they'd eaten, watched a football match on the television while Clare finished wrapping the presents. He always liked to look at the cards they'd received, and she'd shown him the pile before festooning them around the house. He'd read the letters that had come with them, too, but Clare hadn't told him about the letter from Mrs Prizbilski; that, she thought, had really been meant for her, and if she wasn't interested in it then there was no point in showing it to

Boyd. Pausing in wrapping a gift for his mother, she glanced across at him as he sat at ease in his armchair, wearing jeans and a sweater, a drink on the table beside him. Other people had mentioned adoption, but not Boyd. Now it occurred to her for the first time that she had absolutely no idea of his feelings on the subject. But had he kept quiet because he knew hers? Was she being selfish by depriving him of even a second-hand child? The phrase stayed in her mind. Was that why she was so against adoption? Because she instinctively knew that she would never be able to think of someone else's baby as her own?

Clare gazed unseeingly down at the parcel in her hands, trying to think the thing through, to analyse feelings she had never looked into before.

'Gone on strike?'

She glanced up to find Boyd watching her. 'Oh. No, just thinking.'

'What about?'

'Whether I've got two presents mixed up,' she fibbed.

'That isn't like you; you've got a terrific memory.'

'I must be getting old, then.'

'Good, I like older women.'

'Since when?'

'Since now. Why don't you come over here and I'll tell you about it?'

Abandoning the presents, Clare went to sit on his lap, settling comfortably against his shoulder. They kissed a little, talked and laughed a little, then kissed a lot, so that the presents didn't get finished that evening after all—and the right time to tell him about the letter was past.

Christmas was upon them then. Clare drove up to London on the last working day to collect Boyd after the office binge, and the next day they drove to her mother's house, where she had to spend two days in the close company of her brother, his wife and their two very young children. They were boys, the elder one old enough this year to understand what Christmas meant and to be excited about it. He and his brother hung their big, colourful stockings on the bottom of their bed, but were too restless to sleep for ages. It wasn't until midnight that their father crept in with their presents, he and his wife almost as excited about it as their children. Clare could hardly bear to see the happiness in their faces, but Boyd understood, and made her play silly, noisy games and knock back a couple of stiff drinks before they went to bed.

But the children woke early, shrieking with excitement when they found their stockings full of parcels. Clare stirred, disorientated for a moment, but then she remembered and grew tense as she listened. Boyd, too, had woken and he took her into the comfort of his arms, stroked her hair as she cried, then held her until she fell asleep again.

There were more presents under the Christmas tree for the children to open later in the day, but Clare went out into the kitchen to take over the cooking so that her mother could go and watch them instead.

There was no point in driving all the way home again that night, so instead they went directly to Boyd's grandmother's house the next morning. Again there were lots of little children high with excitement as they tore the carefully tied bows and paper from their gifts. And there were already too many women to help with the cooking, so all she could do was to turn away and talk to other childless and single people there. Set apart, different from those other women proudly fussing over their children.

Boxing Day ended at last and they drove home, Clare thankful that it was all over. It seemed like the longest three days in her life, but Boyd had the rest of the week off, which was wonderful. They got home late and went straight to bed, only the next morning sorting out the gifts they had been given and putting them away. Some of the things Clare really appreciated: a year's sub-scription to an antiques magazine from Boyd's mother, and books on her favourite blue and white transfer-printed china from Boyd, as well as tights, underwear, and things that she could use. But there were an awful lot of what she described as 'smellies'; little baskets, sachets, miniature straw hats, pin-cushions and the like, filled with pot-pourri, bath salts and talc, and enough bars of soap to make her think people were trying to tell her something.

Clare packed them all into boxes to be put away while Boyd went through his gifts. He had received three packs of playing cards, which he took over to the bureau to put away. He opened the drawer, reached in, then said, 'What's this?' and pulled out the letter from Mrs Prizbilski.

CHAPTER FOUR

CLARE'S face flushed with colour, making Boyd's eyebrows rise in surprise. 'Oh, that. It's nothing.'

She got quickly to her feet and went to take it from him, but he moved away, his face alert, surprised, frowning. 'It looks as if you weren't very happy at receiving it, from the way it's crumpled.'

'No, I wasn't. Can I have it?' She held out her hand.

Boyd gave it to her, unread, demonstrating his trust in her. But he couldn't resist saying, 'Are you going to tell me who it's from?'

Clare hesitated, folding and refolding the letter. 'It's from Mrs Prizbilski.'

'Mrs——? Oh, yes, I remember. You mean she wrote to you personally?'

'Well, no... I suppose it was to us both, but—but I think she really intended it for me.'

Coming over, Boyd put his arm round her waist. 'But we're a couple, aren't we? A team?'

She nodded and slowly handed him the letter, not sure whether she wanted him to see it or not. Not yet sure enough of her own feelings on the subject to have to accept or do battle with his. Boyd gazed at her averted head for a long moment, then opened the letter and smoothed it out. Going over to the window-seat, he perched on its edge and began to read.

But after only a few moments he said, 'Did you actually manage to decipher this?'

'It gets easier as you go on.'

'I certainly hope so.' He persevered, while Clare sat down in a chair and watched him, her hands twined together, scanning his face for his reactions. But Boyd could be completely inscrutable when he wanted to be, and he chose now not to let any of his feelings show. When he'd read it he folded it again and looked at her. 'So?'

She was immediately irritated. 'What do you mean, "so"? What kind of question is that?'

'It means, why did you crumple up the letter? Why didn't you tell me about it? Have you answered it? What is *your* reaction to what she's written? Is that enough for you?' Boyd's voice had grown cold.

'But I want to know what you think about it,' Clare insisted stubbornly.

'My immediate reaction is the same as yours—throw it away, if the egg-stain on the back means that you chucked it in the rubbish bin,' Boyd returned.

'Yes, I did.'

'But you took it out again.'

'Yes. I—I felt I owed her an answer.'

'Why?' Boyd's tone sounded as if he disagreed.

'She was being kind. Probably thought she was doing a marvellous thing for everyone concerned.'

'And just how did she know that you were unable to have children?'

Clare flushed; she'd forgotten that he would find that out. 'I suppose I must have mentioned it,' she said lamely.

He straightened up and gave the letter back to her.

'Well? What do you think?' Clare asked again, her voice almost pleading.

'I think that you should do as you were going to do— throw it away. The woman had no right even to suggest the idea.'

'No.' Clare looked down at the sheets of notepaper in her hand. 'I don't suppose it would be possible to adopt foreign children anyway.'

Boyd gave her a sharp glance. 'Forget about it, darling,' he said on a rough note. 'Thinking about it will only upset you.'

'Yes, I suppose so. But don't you think I ought to answer the letter?'

With a definite shake of his head Boyd said, 'No, I don't. You didn't ask Mrs Prizbilski to look for——' He broke off, his face tightening. 'You didn't ask her, did you—while you were having your confidential little chat?'

Clare flushed. 'No, of course not. It's entirely her own idea.' Her head came up. 'But I still think I ought to answer it.'

'Then do so—or else hide it away again until you've made up your own mind how to deal with it.' And he gathered up a pile of his presents and took them upstairs.

After that Clare found it impossible to ask Boyd how he felt about adoption. It was certainly something he had never mentioned, so she didn't know whether he had strong feelings about it or not. But then, he had never talked about having children until she had got broody and then pregnant. He'd had to discuss it then, of course. But as far as Clare could remember it had been a very one-sided discussion. She had been so excited at her *fait accompli*, so full of joy, that Boyd had had to accept it. He might have been a bit wry about having had the decision taken out of his hands at first, but he had been OK after that, even if he hadn't exactly gone overboard about becoming a father.

Thinking about it, she wondered if it was something to do with his being an only child. She had a brother that she'd had to share with, even though he was older, but Boyd had been doted on by his parents, especially his mother, and still was. Perhaps he had got used to being the sole recipient of love and didn't know how to share it. But he would make a good father, Clare was confident of that. Having seen him playing ball games with his young male cousins and gravely taking a little girl on his knee to read her a story, she knew that the basic instinct was there. Latent, but definitely there, waiting for his own children to come along to bring it to the surface.

Or perhaps he had been working so hard for this promotion that he had buried all the usual kind of ambitions, like being a parent, Clare mused. Subconsciously he might have seen it as a distraction that could be put off until later, until the right time. What it boiled down to, she supposed, was that he just wasn't ready for fatherhood. Although they had, on her doctor's advice, deliberately gone in for the second baby, and the third. But after the third miscarriage the question of Boyd's paternal feelings had become immaterial, of course. Until now. Until she had received Mrs Prizbilski's letter.

Neither of them referred to the letter again, but Clare put it back in the drawer, unable to throw it away.

They spent the next couple of days doing odd jobs about the house, clearing out the cellar, and hanging new curtains in the second spare bedroom ready for some friends who were coming to stay for New Year's Eve. That bedroom was to have been the nursery, of course, but she had never been pregnant long enough to warrant decorating it for a baby and Clare was glad now that they hadn't; it would have been a torture to strip it all off again.

New Year's Eve was fun. Their friends, a childless couple of their own age, arrived in the morning and they spent the afternoon contriving fancy-dress costumes for

them all to wear to a dance at a local hotel that evening.
The partying went on long into the small hours, but then
they stayed up talking and drinking coffee until the dawn
was breaking before they went to bed, and it was
afternoon before Boyd kissed Clare awake.

'Have I made love to you yet this year?' he murmured
against her neck.

Clare gave a theatrical sigh. '*No one* has made love
to me yet this year.'

'You must feel very deprived. I think that ought to be
put right at once.'

Turning on her side, Clare lay, alongside him. 'I've a
feeling you're about to.'

'Feel all you want,' he invited, and pulled her close
against him.

The holiday over, Boyd plunged back into work, into
his new job. Almost from the first day he was late home
at night, getting to know his new responsibilities, organising his team to chase new markets. When he did
arrive home there was time for little more than to eat
and relax for a couple of hours before they went to bed.
And after a couple of weeks he had to fly to Hong Kong,
and then on to Australia and was away for ten days.
Luckily there were few social events so soon after
Christmas, but Clare had to go to a friend's birthday
party alone. It would have been nicer with Boyd as her
escort but it didn't matter too much as the friend, Angie,
was one she had made through their mutual interest in
blue and white china. Clare took along a pretty plate
with a pastoral scene as a present for her, and Angie was
gratifyingly pleased.

'Oh, that's beautiful! How did you know I was looking
for that pattern?'

'Probably because you happened to let the fact slip
several times,' Clare laughed.

'But how did you find it?'

'I put an ad in an antiques magazine.'

'Clare, you are the kind of friend I don't deserve,' Angie said gratefully.

'Of course you do.' Clare gave her a hug. 'Happy birthday.'

It was some time later before the two girls were able to talk alone again. Clare was standing in front of a set of wall shelves where Angie kept her best pieces, when her friend came to join her. 'Hey, how do you feel about going with me to a weekend seminar for blue and white collectors?'

'I didn't know there were any of those. When is it?'

'Just over a month's time. And it's only about an hour and a half's drive away. The programme sounds really good, too. Look.'

Angie produced a printed leaflet and they went through it together, exclaiming at items that especially interested them. 'You're right, it does,' Clare agreed. 'But a whole weekend—I don't know.'

'Why not? It would be great.'

'Yes, but Boyd might be home. I wouldn't want to go away and leave him.'

'He leaves you, doesn't he?'

'Yes, but that's work; he doesn't have any choice.'

'He went away to play in that squash tournament, didn't he?'

'Yes, but I could have gone with him if I'd been well enough.' The tournament had taken place when she was recovering from a miscarriage and she had insisted that Boyd go, although he had offered to stay at home. But he had played as hard for his place in the team as he had worked for his promotion, and there'd been no way she was going to let him give it up.

Angie ignored her. 'And he might well be away himself that weekend.'

'Yes, but he might not.'

'Stop saying "yes, but". Come on, Clare, you know you'll enjoy it, and I don't want to be alone among all those strangers. Come with me, *please*.'

Clare hesitated a moment, glanced at the array of plates on the shelves and then capitulated. 'OK. I really would like to go.'

'Great! I'll send off the booking form first thing tomorrow.'

'So that I don't have a chance to change my mind,' Clare laughed.

It was while Boyd was away that Clare finally wrote to Mrs Prizbilski. It was a very difficult letter to write, and she screwed up nearly a whole pad of aborted efforts before she'd finished. In the end she kept her answer very brief, thanking the Polish woman for her suggestion but saying that she and Boyd had no plans to adopt a child. After Mrs Prizbilski's long, chatty letter it seemed so short as to be almost rude, which wasn't what Clare wanted, but she couldn't think of anything to add that would keep the letter impersonal. In the end she just put 'Thank you again for your interest, Love, Clare', and left it at that, fervently hoping the older woman would get the message and not write to her again.

Writing the letter had been hard, but Clare found that pushing the thought of the orphaned twins out of her mind was even harder, so she, too, plunged back into work. With Boyd away, she was able to paint almost at her leisure, working, eating and sleeping when she felt like it, instead of being governed by Boyd's schedule. Sometimes, when she became really engrossed, she worked far into the night, living on soup and sandwiches, the silent, empty house warm and comfortable around her. Then she would get up late, and go for a brisk walk round the village or across the frost-layered fields before starting work again. Clare missed Boyd, of course, but didn't find the solitude at all oppressive; she felt like an animal that had hibernated for the winter, resting up before the busy season ahead. Before the seasonal round of company entertaining started again, Clare thought wryly. She had no enthusiasm for it; if anything, these ten days of living her own life, of being completely independent, were turning her even more against being the sales director's dutiful wife.

It was, Clare reflected, the first time that she had been really alone for any length of time in her life. Before her marriage she had lived at home with her mother, not even going away to art college because she had lived within daily travelling distance. Since her marriage Boyd had been away on conferences and things, but never for as long as this, and she had quite often taken the opportunity to go to stay with her mother or friends. It was a new sensation, being responsible only for her own life like this, and Clare found it rather a heady experience.

Not that she was completely cut off from the outside, of course. Boyd phoned her every evening, and both her mother and Boyd's called several times and also invited her to stay, both of which invitations she refused, fortunately able to legitimately plead fears of frozen tanks and burst pipes if she left the house during this icy weather. They called so regularly that Clare began to suspect that Boyd had instructed them to do so, but couldn't resent his thinking about her and trying to take care of her while he was away.

Other friends rang too, of course: Angie to say that they were definitely booked in for the weekend seminar and that she would drive. 'I've got a problem, though,'

she told Clare. 'You know that beautiful big bowl I
bought; the one that isn't marked? Well, I thought I'd
take it down to the seminar to have the experts identify
it, but it's so large that I'm afraid it might get broken.
I've tried to photograph it but it didn't come out well
because of the shape. Do you think you could do a sketch
of the pattern so I could take that instead?'

'Of course. Tell you what; why don't you bring it over
this evening and I'll do it then?'

'Great. I'll get Ian to give me a lift over so that we
can have a drink.'

'Come to dinner?' Clare invited.

'Better not; Ian hates eating alone.'

Another woman whose life was bound by her husband's likes and dislikes, Clare realised. 'How are you
going to manage to get away on this weekend if Ian
doesn't like being left alone?' she asked when Angie arrived that evening.

'Oh, that's OK. He's been wanting to go and stay with
an old college friend of his who lives in the Lake District.
They go hill-walking,' Angie explained with a grimace.

'Weren't you invited?'

'Definitely not. His friend is a bachelor.'

'Oh, that explains it.'

They both laughed and opened the wine that Clare
had chilling in the fridge. Their shared hobby was their
first topic of conversation, broken off when Clare took
a call from Boyd. He was in Australia now, and there
was the smallest pause between her speaking and his reply
as their voices covered the thousands of miles.

Angie said hello to him before he rang off, then said
to Clare, 'I envy you, having Boyd as a husband. He's
so thoughtful as well as being good-looking.'

'I'm sure Ian is just as thoughtful,' Clare said lightly, not wanting to be drawn into personal confidences. Angie was her friend, but on a different level.

To her relief, Angie laughed. 'Yes, I suppose he is really. We've been married so long that I think we just take each other for granted nowadays, that's all.'

'How long have you been married?'

'Nearly eight years. Perhaps I've got the proverbial seven-year itch.'

'That's how long we've been married,' Clare said thoughtfully.

They looked at each other and laughed, but it was an uneasy laughter. Quickly Clare refilled their glasses and Angie unpacked her bowl from its box. 'Can you do the sketch, do you think?'

'Yes, I can copy the outline but it's such a deep blue that you really need to show the colour, too.' She thought for a moment as she examined the bowl. 'What if I copied the scene in paints rather than just sketched it?'

'That sounds a marvellous idea, but I don't want you to spend too much time on it, Clare; I know how busy you are.'

'As a matter of fact, I've been able to catch up with my work while Boyd's been away. I've even been able to experiment with some new ideas that I'll try to sell. So I'll have plenty of time to do this if you don't mind leaving it with me.'

'No, of course not. I'm grateful.' Angie took a long drink of her wine. 'I wish I were self-employed like you,' she said wistfully. 'I'm sick to death of working in an office all day. Stuck in a room by myself with a window that only looks out on to a lorry-loading bay.'

'Can't you change your office?'

Angie shook her head. 'I'm stuck there so long as I'm at that firm.'

'So change your job.'

'I've thought about it, but it would really only be changing from one job I don't enjoy to another. I'd like to give up office work altogether if I could, but I don't know anything else.'

'You know about blue and white china,' Clare remarked.

'Yes, that's true. But I can hardly make a living out of that.'

'Why not?' An idea came into Clare's mind and she sat forward eagerly. 'Other people make money out of dealing in antique china, so why shouldn't you?'

'You mean, open an antique shop?' Angie stared at her. 'I couldn't possibly.'

'No, not a shop—but you could have a stall at antiques markets.'

'But you need loads of stock for that. You have to go round to auctions and buy cheap so that you can sell the goods on. And I can never get to auctions because they're always on during the week when I'm at work.'

'But you won't be stuck in the office, will you?' Clare pointed out. 'Going to auctions will be part of your work, your new job.'

Angie stared at her then shook her head. 'It's impossible. I'd need capital to start and all ours went on Ian's new car. And most of our wages goes on paying off the mortgage.'

'But you have your collection of blue and white,' Clare pointed out.

'You mean—you mean, sell it?' Angie stared again, her eyes disbelieving.

'Not all of it, just a few of your lesser pieces. And you must have loads of ordinary stuff at home you don't want,' Clare said, thinking of the boxes of unwanted gifts in her own loft. 'You could go to a car-boot sale and raise money from that.'

'Well, yes, I could. But leave work...' Angie's voice was heavy with self-doubt.

'I suppose it comes down to how badly you want to leave. If you're content to stay as you are, working in an office.'

'It's all right for you.' There was a faint hint of resentment in Angie's tone. 'You've got Boyd behind you. It probably wouldn't matter if you didn't work at all.'

'It would matter to me,' Clare said sharply. 'I left work to take up painting when we could hardly afford it, but I felt that it was something I had to do. OK, so Boyd was willing to help me if necessary, but he hasn't had to. I don't make anything like the money I was earning in London, of course, but I have no fares, I don't have to spend a fortune on working clothes, and I'm a hell of a lot happier.'

Angie blinked, then laughed and took a long drink of her wine. 'Wow, you really got going there. I'm sorry, I didn't mean to put you down.'

'And you mustn't put yourself down either. You're sensible and intelligent, Angie; if you really want to do this then you'll make a success of it.' Clare laughed. 'After all, people have been making a profit out of all the china you've bought over the years; now you could make a living selling to other people.'

Holding out her glass, Angie said, 'Is there any more wine? I think I need it. It's a wonderful idea,' she said sincerely. 'But what about Ian?'

'What about him?'

'Well, for a start, antiques fairs are always held at the weekend; I couldn't just leave him alone. And he insists on having a proper Sunday lunch.'

'So encourage him to go walking more often, or take him with you, get him interested in helping you. You never know, he might enjoy it.'

Angie didn't look as if she could imagine that, but she said, 'I don't suppose it would be every weekend. And I might be able to get a part-time job, just working a couple of days a week.'

'Now you're beginning to think,' Clare said with a grin.

'And if it doesn't work out I could always get another permanent office job.'

'I'm going to pretend I didn't hear you say that. It's defeatist. You will succeed, and though you won't make a fortune you won't be tied to a desk all day. You'll be out meeting people, buying, selling, learning more all the time. You'll be in control of your own life, doing what you want to do instead of what you think you have to.'

Angie took another long drink. 'Either this wine is going to my head or all your ideas are, because I feel as if my brain is buzzing.' She raised glitteringly excited eyes to meet Clare's. 'I think you may have just changed my life.' Reaching out, she touched Clare's hand. 'But will you help me? Just at first. I'd be so nervous, standing behind a stall on my own.'

'Of course. I'll help all I can. It will be fun.'

They discussed the idea some more, but her husband arrived not long afterwards to take Angie home. 'You two seem to have had a good evening,' he remarked, looking at their flushed cheeks and sparkling eyes. 'What was it—girl-talk?'

His wife looked at him, gave a small smile, and said, 'No, woman-talk,' and walked ahead of him to the car.

It snowed overnight, the white blanket thick around the house when Clare looked out the next morning. The cottage was in a lane that led from their village to the next, but in the opposite direction from the main road, so no snow-ploughs came to clear the snow that day, although the paper-boy, the milkman and the postman all struggled valiantly through on foot. Clare spent the morning carefully copying the colours and scene on Angie's bowl, but in the afternoon, when the sun came out for a couple of hours, she took her sketch-book and went out to find some winter scenes. There were too many of them; she ended up taking lots of photographs and making dozens of sketches that she could develop later.

The afternoon in the open air did her good. She came home filled with enthusiasm, determined to try for new markets. She decided to put together a new portfolio and take it round to all the publishers of children's books. That would be OK; she felt strong enough to do children's paintings now. Maybe I'm getting over the miscarriage at last, she thought, and was glad to feel normal again.

Angie, too, was still full of enthusiasm when she rang that night. 'I'm so excited that I've hardly been able to work today. I've been trying to think things through financially, and I've decided to stay on at work until the end of March so that I can save as much money as I can. And I'll do the car-boot sale as soon as possible so that the money will earn some interest. There's one being held in a couple of weeks' time that I'm going to try for.'

'That's a good idea. I've got loads of things you can have.'

'Thanks, Clare, but I couldn't let you do that,' Angie said firmly. 'I want to do this by my own efforts. But by all means come along and sell your stuff on the stall.'

Clare was about to refuse, but yet another idea came into her head—it was all ideas these last couple of days—and she said, 'Maybe I will. There's a project I would like to donate some money to.' She put the phone down, thinking that maybe the little Polish twins would appreciate some new clothes and toys, things that she could buy with the proceeds from the car-boot sale. Surely no one—even Boyd—could object to that?

The weather grew cold in the night, and the next morning when she awoke the sky was dark and grey and there was a cold north wind that howled round the house and made the windows rattle. There would be no pleasure in going out today. Clare turned up the central heating and went up to the loft to sort out some things she could sell. At the back of the loft there were a couple of dozen boxes of stuff that hadn't been unpacked since they'd moved into the house. Pushing later additions out of the way, Clare went to those boxes first, finding lampshades and light fittings that were too modern for the cottage, curtains that didn't fit, clothes they no longer wore, wedding and Christmas gifts they'd never used, string-tied bundles of old books—and a box of brand-new baby clothes.

Sitting down on the dusty floor, Clare slowly drew them out. They had been bought during the couple of months of euphoria during her first pregnancy. She hadn't exactly forgotten them, rather deliberately put them out of her mind. She hadn't gone in for pretty, lacy stuff; these were all bright and colourful things for a with-it, fashionable child. Clothes she hadn't been able to resist buying and Boyd had put away during her depression after the miscarriage. She went through them now, forcing herself not to get upset, trying to think which she could bear to part with, which would be suitable to send to Poland.

Suddenly Clare bundled them all back in the box, deciding to pack up the whole lot; it would be stupid to leave them here in memory of her lost baby when they could be useful elsewhere. She should have got rid of them long ago. Bringing all the things down to her studio, Clare parcelled up the baby clothes and began sticking price tags on the things she'd decided to sell. About noon it began to snow again, a real blizzard that soon built up on the earlier layer of snow and made the sky so dark that she had to turn on the lights. There were quite a few things that she wasn't sure how to price, so Clare decided to leave them and discuss it with Angie. Going into the kitchen, she heated some soup and began to make a sandwich. The lights flickered and went out, then came on again. But after a few minutes they flickered several more times and then went out completely.

For several minutes Clare stood in the kitchen, looking up at the light bulb, confidently expecting it to come on again. But her soup was going cold, so she quickly ate it, then put on her warmest clothes and boots, grabbed a shovel and went outside to clear the snow from the back door to the store where they kept their pile of logs for the fire. She made several journeys, lighting the fire in the sitting-room and being careful to let as little cold air into the house as possible. Then she found candles and an old oil lamp and closed all the shutters and curtains, trying to keep the place warm, scared that the pipes might freeze.

It would have been helpful if there had been some warning of the power cut, she thought ruefully, and then realised that she could still phone up the electricity board to find out how long it was likely to last. But when she picked up the phone that, too, was dead. Another modern invention that had been unable to withstand the fierceness of the storm, presumably. All the rest of that

day Clare waited for the power to come back on. At one
point she thought of walking down to the village, but it
was too cold and the snow was getting too deep.
Retreating into the cosiness of the house like a rabbit
into its hole, she turned on her battery-operated radio
and heard that the bad weather had set in all over the
country and was likely to go on for a couple more days.

Sitting on the settee in front of the fire, Clare laughed,
feeling suddenly excited. It would be like going back to
when the house was built. It would be fun. That night
she cooked her supper on the fire, and lit another in her
bedroom, but it went out in the night and she woke up
feeling cold and had to get up and put on a load more
clothes. The blizzard had blown itself out by the next
morning, but it was still very cold and there was no paper-
boy, milkman or postman that day. Clare went out to
get more logs and stood still, suddenly aware of the intense silence all around her, the snow deadening all
sound. She shivered and went quickly back inside. The
bad weather lasted for three more days, days in which
Clare was able to work at her table drawn close up to
the window, fingerless gloves on her hands, to read by
candle-light, and lie in bed and listen to the radio until
the battery ran out.

She felt, then, rather like a hermit, shut away in his
cell so that he could concentrate only on spiritual things.
And, like a hermit's, this became a time of introspection
for Clare. A retreat into herself. What do I want out of
life, she thought, now that I can't have children? But it
was easier to know what she didn't want. She certainly
didn't want to resume her career and go back to work
in London. And she didn't want to spend more time
than she absolutely had to at corporate entertainment
functions for Boyd's company. Well, it would be easy
enough to persuade Boyd that she would be happier

working at home, even though he wanted her to paint only as a hobby, but she knew that she would have a battle on her hands if she tried to opt out of being a company wife. I advised Angie to take control of her own life when I don't even have control of my own, she thought wryly.

Boyd was often in her thoughts. She still loved him, of course, that went without saying, but she felt that they had both changed; she certainly had. Perhaps it was only her, though. Perhaps her values and ambitions had changed while Boyd's had stayed on the same course, become more intense. And now that he had come close to achieving his ambitions she no longer wished to share them. Lord, life was ironical sometimes. But she hadn't lost all ambition; she still wanted to make a commercial success of her painting, if she could. Boyd probably thought that she was being selfish and disloyal, but she felt that she had a right to her own life, a right to change and want other things, have other interests that would have to grow and be strong enough to take the place of the children she couldn't have. Clare's mind fixed on this and became full of strong, stubborn determination. When Boyd comes home, she decided, we're going to have to talk, to work out some ground rules, because I refuse to spend my life being at the beck and call of his company any longer!

A couple of pipes had frozen when she got up one morning, but Clare went up into the loft and managed to unfreeze them with the help of a battery-powered hair-drier she unearthed from the back of the bathroom cupboard. Hearing them unblock and the water run through gave her a big sense of achievement. I can cope, she thought. I can manage on my own. Another morning, when the snow had stopped and the sun came out again, there was a shout outside and she ran to the door. The farmer who lived half a mile further down the lane stood in the road, the snow almost up to his waist.

'You all right, Mrs Russell?'

'Yes, thanks. I'm fine.'

'Is your husband there? Did he make it home all right?'

Clare laughed. 'He's in Australia; probably basking in the sun.'

The farmer laughed too, but said, 'We've got a generator going up at the farm; do you want to come and stay with us until the power's back on?'

'That's very kind of you but I'm managing very well.'

'I don't like to think of you being here alone.'

'But I'm fine, really.'

He nodded. 'We'll be trying to clear the road with the tractor later on today.'

'Great. I'll have a stiff whisky waiting for you.'

When he'd gone Clare put on her outdoor clothes and cleared the path from the front door to the gate. The wind had died completely now and the sun was dazzling as it reflected off the snow. Looking up at the sky, Clare felt suddenly happy and content. I haven't been bored or lonely even without the telephone or television, she thought. Even without Boyd. I can live from within myself. It was a moment of discovery and self-knowledge. It made her feel that she was growing from being a girl into a woman, from being a wife reliant on her husband into an independently minded person. But whether that was a good thing or a bad, she wasn't at all sure.

When she heard the sound of the tractor coming Clare went out to the gate, carrying a tray with a bottle of whisky and some glasses. The farmer had an earth-mover fixed to the front of the powerful tractor and this was clearing a wide but slow sweep down the lane. He and his son were glad of the whisky and stayed to rest for about ten minutes before pushing on. Clare watched them for a while then went back to the house. When she opened the door she heard the phone ringing. The lines must have been mended. Trust the authorities to get the phones mended before the electricity. She could have run to answer it, but Clare stopped to take off her wet boots and put on her indoor shoes, then walked leisurely over to the phone. She lifted her hand to answer it—but it stopped.

It would only have been her mother checking to see if she was all right, Clare thought in a mixture of guilt and relief. Either that or Boyd's mother, carrying out his instructions. Maybe tonight I'll phone them both. Or maybe not; if they know the electricity is still off they'll insist I go and stay with one or other of them. It didn't cross her mind that it might be Boyd; it was the wrong time for a call from Australia.

But the phone call and the farmer with his tractor had shattered the feeling of isolation. The road was open and she could walk down to the village shop, where she could not only buy some supplies, but also hear all the local snow stories and catch up on the gossip. And she would be able to buy a paper and learn what had been happening in the rest of the world during her days of snowbound seclusion. But if she had been cut off then the whole of the village probably had as well, so there might not be any fresh food or newspapers. It was a convenient excuse, one that made Clare feel less guilty about leaving it until tomorrow.

That afternoon she again worked on the sketches she had drawn when the snow first fell, putting all her talent into a painting of an old, leaning wooden post, hung with a broken-off piece of twisted barbed-wire, that rose from a snowdrift. It was a simple subject, but something about the arrangement of the weathered timber and the sharp wire against the snow had caught her imagination, and when Clare sat back she was satisfied that she had put her fascination into the picture.

Only now that it was finished did she realise that the light was almost gone and the studio was very chilly. There was a fireplace in the room and she had lit a fire earlier, but only a small one because the supply of logs was getting low. It had gone out without her noticing. So instead Clare lit the fire in the sitting-room and put a now blackened kettle on the trivet above it to boil, and a large potato in the ashes to bake. Some of the water she put into a vacuum flask for a hot drink before she went to bed, the rest she used to wash with, adding cold water to make it go further. Lots of hot water was the thing she missed most, Clare decided, and thought longingly of a bath full of scented bubbles.

She put more water on to boil to fill her hot-water bottles and went into the kitchen to open her last tin of soup, to light the candles and the lamp. Carrying the lamp, she went into the sitting-room—and almost dropped it as a swath of light suddenly lit the room. For a moment she thought that the electricity had come back on, but then the lights passed on and she heard the sound of an engine. It was a car going past the house, the first in nearly a week. But then the car stopped near by and there was silence. Suddenly feeling very much alone, Clare put down the lamp and picked up the poker, then remembered that the front door wasn't bolted and hurried into the hall. The door opened before she could reach it and she raised the metal rod to defend herself against the hooded figure in the black parka that stepped inside.

CHAPTER FIVE

'Is THAT any way to greet your husband?'

At the sound of Boyd's amused voice Clare dropped the poker and ran into his arms. 'Boyd!' He hugged her tightly but then she pushed him away. 'Hey, you're all wet.'

'I had to dig myself out of the snow about six times.'

He closed the door and took off the parka, then pulled her to him again to kiss her properly. 'Is that better?' he asked when he finally let her go.

'Much. My, you have been away a long time.'

'It notices, huh?'

'Definitely.'

Boyd grinned, then shivered. 'It's freezing in here.'

'Come into the sitting-room, it's much warmer in there.' She pulled him into the room and closed the curtains, got him a brandy and sat him down in a chair in front of the fire. Then she gave him a puzzled look. 'Aren't you supposed to be in Australia?'

'I was due back two days ago.'

'Really?' She thought back. 'Yes, I suppose you were. I've lost track of the days.'

'Actually I came back a day early. I'd read in the papers about this area being cut off and I was worried about you when I couldn't get through on the phone. But when I got back to England I found the roads were impassable and I just couldn't get to you, so I've been sitting it out in a hotel in the nearest town, waiting for the weather to break.' He pulled her down on to his lap.

'I've been worrying myself silly about you. Have you been here alone all the time?'

'Yes, but I've been fine. I'm sorry you worried.'

'I hoped you'd gone to stay with one of the parents. Didn't you have a chance to get away?'

'Probably, but I was afraid of the pipes bursting; I didn't want the house to be flooded.'

'You should have gone. It must have been hell here without any electricity.'

Clare laughed. 'No, it was fun. Like a camping holiday.'

Boyd's eyebrows rose. 'Have I been worrying for nothing, then?'

'Yes, you have. I managed perfectly well.'

'And the pipes didn't freeze?'

'Yes, they did, but I unblocked them with a hair-drier,' she told him, her voice full of confident triumph.

Boyd gave a wry grin. 'And there was I, foolishly imagining you being half-starved if you hadn't already frozen to death. I've been making life hell for all the authorities concerned, demanding to know when they were going to clear the roads, when they were going to get the power and the phone lines fixed.'

'You stamped your foot, huh?'

'And some. But when the phones were finally fixed and I rang you earlier today there was no reply. That's when I really started to tear my hair.'

Clare straightened up. 'That was you?'

'You mean you heard it and you didn't answer?' Boyd stared at her incredulously.

'It stopped before I could reach it,' she expained, suppressing a pang of mental guilt. 'I was out in the road having a drink with the farmer and his son to celebrate getting the lane clear.'

Boyd groaned. 'And I imagined you lying dead on the floor.'

'Dear idiot.' She kissed him. 'Have another brandy.'

'Thanks. You must have been bored out of your mind.'

'No. Not at all. I've been painting. I've caught up with all my work, thought up loads of new ideas, and even done some pictures.'

The enthusiasm in her voice made him give her a searching look. 'You don't sound as if you've missed me at all.'

Clare chuckled. 'Of course I have—I've used up nearly all the logs you chopped for the fire!'

He smiled, but his eyes were still on her face. 'What else did you do?'

'Not much. I went to bed when it got dark and didn't get up until it was light again.'

'If you spent that much time in bed I should certainly have been here.'

'You certainly should.' Stroking her hand down his face, she kissed him. 'You shouldn't have worried. I can take care of myself.'

Boyd's brows flickered. 'You said that very definitely.'

'I've had plenty of time to find it out. Plenty of time to think.'

Her tone, and the eyes that met his were coolly confident, almost challenging. Boyd gave a small sigh. 'Now why do I think that sounds ominous?'

She laughed and got to her feet. 'I'll fix something to eat and you can tell me all about Australia. Did you see a koala bear?'

'There weren't that many of them roaming around Sydney. I'll go and get my luggage out of the car.' When he came back he said, 'What's for dinner?'

'Soup, steak and sausages—cooked in wine because I put the last of the oil in the lamp—half a baked potato, stir-fry vegetables, and ice-cream to follow.'

'You're living better than I've been. Hasn't the food in the freezer gone off?'

'No, it's so cold in the laundry-room that it hasn't made any difference. The soup's ready.'

They sat down at the table to eat and Boyd told her of his problems in trying to reach her. 'The hardest part was probably when I got back to Heathrow Airport and tried to find the car. The whole of the car park was under about three feet of snow. I knew which section I'd left the car in, of course, but I had to go all along the lines, wiping the snow off every number plate before I could find it and even start to dig it out. And the roads were terrible; cars abandoned, lorries jackknifed across the carriageways. It took me over four hours to do six miles, so I pulled into a pub that put me up for the night. The next day it was better and I was able to reach the county town, but that was as far as I could get. I had to wait until today, when they finally cleared the road into the village. I was right behind the snow-plough.'

'Poor Boyd, you've had a worse time than I've had. And I suppose you left lovely hot weather behind in Australia?'

They talked of his trip through the rest of the meal, then Clare washed the plates in cold water as quickly as she could; the kitchen was too cold to linger in. She carried the lamp up to their bedroom but while they were undressing the light from it dimmed and died. 'That was the last of the oil,' she said regretfully. 'I'll have to go down to the shop tomorrow to try and get some more.'

'Why didn't you go today?' Boyd queried. 'If the tractor cleared the road this morning you must have had time.'

'I didn't want to. The sun was bright and I wanted to paint today.'

They got into bed, the chill taken off by the hot-water bottles, and Boyd drew her close. 'You've got almost as many clothes on as you had before you undressed,' he complained.

'It was cold in bed by myself.'

'Well, I'm here now, so take something off.' She struggled to remove a sweater and he said, 'That's better.' He kissed her throat and Clare snuggled against him, expecting him to make love, but Boyd stroked her hair off her face and said softly into the darkness, 'I've a feeling you've changed since I've been away.'

'How could I have changed in so short a time?'

'I don't know—but I expect I'll find out.'

Clare moved against him. 'There are some things that definitely haven't changed.'

'Really? Then why don't you show me?'

'My pleasure, sir.'

'Mine too, I hope.'

The power came back on during the night. Clare woke in the morning to a warm room and the now strange sound of the pump sending the hot water round. A bath at last! was her first thought. She moved and realised that Boyd was behind her; that, too, felt almost strange. Sliding out of bed, she made for the bathroom, discarding pyjamas, bed-socks and mittens along the way. The water was hot enough. Great. Clare poured in almost a whole bottle of bath foam and got in as soon as she turned on the taps, watching with sybaritic pleasure as the water crept over her legs and up her body. Not until the bath was full did she turn them off and wash her hair, scrub herself all over, then lie back and just luxuriate.

It was almost an hour later when Boyd came in. 'I can hardly see for steam. How long have you been in there?'

'Ages. I may never get out.'

'In that case I may as well join you. Move up.' He climbed in at the other end and leaned back. They didn't have a tap end; when they'd moved here and had a new bathroom suite put in Boyd had insisted that they have a bath with taps in the middle because he was fed up with leaning against them. 'When did the electricity come back on?'

'In the night some time. It's absolutely wonderful to feel clean again. And I'll be able to wash my clothes and clean up the house.' Clare smiled. 'The big advantage of having only candle-light is that you can't see the dirt.'

'I thought you said you were going to stay in here for ages yet?'

'There's work to be done.'

She got up on to her knees, but Boyd also came up on to his and caught her round the waist. 'There's something else that needs to be done first.'

'Again?' She pretended to be shocked.

'I have been away for almost two whole weeks, and I have a great deal of catching up to do,' he told her purposefully, and pulled her close.

The water was almost cold when they finally got out. They dressed quickly and Clare ran downstairs, turning off lights, adjusting timers and clocks, full of energy. She spent the whole morning washing and cleaning, while Boyd made a great many business phone calls before sawing more wood and widening the path she'd cleared to the gate. At lunchtime they went down to the village, calling in at the pub, where they heard about everyone's adventures in the snow and added their own, then on to the shop to buy some food, but, 'I'm afraid there isn't much in,' the woman who ran the store apologised. 'I've only got what was here before we got snowed up, and most of that's gone. But the suppliers have assured me that they'll try and get a van-load here some time today.'

'We may as well go back to the pub and wait,' Boyd decided.

Other people had the same idea, and the afternoon developed into a party until the van arrived at last and they all formed a laughing chain to unload it. Then they queued to buy fresh bread and vegetables, milk and cheese, and trudged home again with bulging shopping bags.

'We'll have a feast tonight with all this,' Clare said happily as she put the food away. 'This bread smells delicious. I made some while you were away and it was OK, but I ran out of flour.' She became aware that Boyd was watching her in some amusement. 'It's all right for you; you've probably been eating your head off at the company's expense while I was snowed up.'

Coming up behind her, he put his hands on her waist. 'It wasn't all right for me, Clare. And I don't want you to have to go through that again—or me, for that matter. As soon as the weather clears we'll put the house up for sale and move back to London.'

'No!' Her reply was instantaneous. She swung round to face him. 'Definitely not. I love this house and I don't want to move.'

'You were cut off and alone. Supposing you'd slipped on the ice out by the wood-shed and broken your leg; you could have frozen to death before anyone found you.'

'That's purely hypothetical. I could just as easily slip off a pavement in London and fall under a bus.'

'I don't like to think of you here alone while I'm away.'

'I'd be alone when you went away wherever I was.'

'You know what I mean, Clare,' Boyd said, his tone hardening.

'I'm not moving,' she said vehemently. 'I can work well here.'

'So your work comes first, does it?'

'No, you come first—but my work is a very close second, so don't *push* it.'

She faced up to him, eyes determined, ready to do battle, but Boyd knew when it was useless to pursue an open attack and he merely gave an amused grin. 'OK. OK. I get the message. Can I do anything to help or shall I go and unpack my stuff?'

'Why don't you unpack while I make an early dinner?'

'Fine.' He went upstairs but came down later with a box, which he handed to her just before dinner. 'Present for you,' he said laconically.

Inside was a gorgeous outfit of a short-sleeved linen jacket in a burnt-orange colour with matching Bermuda shorts and espadrilles, and a silk sleeveless top to go under the jacket in a paler shade of orange. 'Boyd, they're gorgeous! Thank you so much. You know exactly what I like.'

She ran upstairs to carefully hang the clothes in her wardrobe and thanked him again when they sat down to dinner. 'You'll have to take me somewhere snazzy so that I can wear them,' she teased him.

'How about Henley? That snazzy enough for you?'

'You mean Henley Regatta week? Sounds ideal. Will you be able to get a day off to go?'

Boyd's lips twitched. 'No need; the company are having a hospitality tent there on the second day of the regatta.'

Clare stopped eating to raise her head and give him an old-fashioned look. 'I should have known. I really fell for that one, didn't I? Now I can't possibly say that I don't want to go.'

'You'll enjoy it,' Boyd encouraged her. 'We've never been there.'

'Possibly—but I've an idea that we won't get to see much of the rowing.'

'I'll insist that you have a grandstand seat,' he assured her.

They'd finished their first course and were eating the Cornish pasty that she'd cooked, when Boyd said, 'I was talking to the managing director earlier and he said that he's arranged a series of cocktail parties especially to introduce me to customers I haven't yet met. Their wives have been invited along, and so have you, of course. In fact, they want you to act as the hostess, which is quite a compliment.'

'Is it?' Clare said drily. 'When are they?'

He took his diary from his pocket. 'The first one is quite soon, a week on Saturday. And then the next one is a week later, again on the Saturday. The third one is three weeks after that. That's all they've arranged for the moment.'

'What dates are they?' He told her and Clare said, 'I can make the third one, but not the first two.'

'Why on earth not?'

'I've already arranged to go out with Angie.'

Boyd made an impatient sound. 'I suppose this is just a rebellion because I got you to agree to go to Henley.'

'No, it isn't; I would go if I was free. The dates are already down on the engagement calendar. Look, if you don't believe me.'

'What have you arranged to do?'

'Angie has decided to go into business on her own.' Clare explained her friend's plans. 'So she's going to try to raise some capital at a car-boot sale and I promised to help her,' she finished.

'Sell things at a stall?' Boyd was horrified. 'You can't possibly.'

'Don't be such a snob! Of course I can—and I'm going to.'

'It's demeaning.'

'Rubbish!'

'That's what you'll be selling! Angie had no right to involve you in this.'

'She has every right; she's my friend.'

'And I'm your husband and I want you with me. So I think I may just have the greater right,' he said curtly.

Clare's face tightened. 'I have a previous engagement, which I intend to keep. And just for the record, Boyd, in future I will only attend your company functions when it suits me to do so. They employ you, not me, and I'm not going to just stop working, or going out with my friends, because they arbitrarily decide that that's when they want me. Given sufficient notice, and if I'm not doing anything, then I will be happy to go wherever they want. But those are my terms, Boyd.'

'Terms? Is this a war, then?' He was glaring at her across the table, his food hardly touched. 'I knew something like this was going to happen. I was right when I said you've changed.'

'If you mean that I've decided to take control of my own life, then yes, I have changed.'

'And what about me?'

'You already control your own life. If you love me you won't try to stop me doing the same with mine.'

He gave an angry snort. 'Don't try that kind of emotional blackmail on me.'

'Why not? You're always doing it to me. You're doing it right now.'

Boyd's jaw hardened. 'I need your support, Clare.'

'You have it,' she replied immediately. 'If your company had contacted me and told me about these cocktail parties I could have told them I wasn't free on those dates and asked them to change them. But they went ahead and expect me to obediently fall in with their plans. Well, I won't. They can find someone else to act as their hostess or change the dates to suit me.'

'They can't do that, the invitations have already gone out.' Clare shrugged, and Boyd leaned forward to say angrily, 'You seem to forget that your phone has been cut off; they couldn't contact you.'

'Did they try?'

It was obvious that Boyd didn't know. Swiftly changing tactics, he said, 'Is this car-boot sale with Angie so important? Couldn't she manage on her own?'

'No, she's nervous. I've promised to go with her.'

'Couldn't she postpone it till another day?'

'No, she's already sent off her fee. And she wants to do it as soon as possible so that she can earn some interest.' She saw from Boyd's expression what he was going to say, so quickly added fiercely, 'And don't you *dare* suggest giving her some money just so that I don't have to go.'

His lips thinned. 'When does it finish?'

'Not till four. There's no way I could get home, change, and get up to London in time if your party starts at six o'clock; that's the usual time for cocktails, isn't it?'

Boyd nodded, and tapped the table impatiently. 'There should be some way we can compromise on this. Perhaps Angie wouldn't mind if you left early? She should have got over her nervousness after a couple of hours or so, surely?'

Clare hesitated. She didn't really want to ask Angie in case her friend thought that she'd changed her mind and wanted to get out of it, which she definitely didn't. So she said, 'I won't ask her. But I will go in my own car and if we've sold everything or if I think it will be OK to leave Angie on her own then I'll come back early and try to get to the party.'

'Very generous,' Boyd commented sarcastically.

'I don't have to do even that,' she shot back.

He gave her a grim look, but said, 'All right, I'll accept that. Now, what about the next party? What's happening then—another car-boot sale?'

'No, I'm going away for the weekend.'

'Are you, indeed?'

'Yes, to a seminar on blue and white china.'

'And I suppose it didn't occur to you to check with me before you made the booking?'

'You were away. You also said you were going to be away a lot in future.'

'All the more reason to check first whether I was going to be at home that weekend.'

She gave him a stony look. 'Am I supposed to turn down everything just in case you might be home? Anyway, you forget; the phone wasn't working.'

'You don't get away with that one, Clare; it must have been working when you made the reservation.'

'Angie made it.'

'Angie seems to have a lot to answer for.' He pushed his plate away. 'This food is cold. You've ruined my first meal back at home.'

'And you've ruined the first decent meal I've had in a week.'

Boyd's brows drew into a frown. 'We're going to go on clashing over this, aren't we?'

'Not if you agree to my terms. And it's to your own advantage; at least, then, I'll go willingly to the company functions instead of feeling that I've been dragged along against my wishes and resenting every minute.'

He gave her a considering look, then appeared to decide that there was no way he was going to dissuade her. 'The board isn't going to like it.'

'Then it's about time that the board dragged itself into the modern era and realised that women have their own lives to lead and they're no longer content with just being company wives!'

Boyd's cold hazel eyes showed the opposite emotions to her defiant green ones. 'And just how far does leading your own life go?' he asked gratingly.

Her cheeks flushed. 'I love you. That hasn't changed and it never will.' Her gaze met his steadily, in clear-eyed assurance.

After a moment Boyd nodded. 'Well, I suppose that's something. All right, Miss Independent, I agree to your terms. Is there any pudding?'

'Of course.' Clare gave him a dazzling smile, thinking her battle won, and rushed to clear away the uneaten food and bring the next course.

The car-boot sale was an unforgettable experience. Earlier, she and Angie had spent anxious hours worrying about how much they should charge and carefully pricing everything. 'I've persuaded Ian to let us borrow his wall-paper-pasting table, and I've got a nice green cloth we can put over it,' Angie told her. 'That should show the things off, especially if we put some boxes on the table to give height.'

It took some time for them to pack the car, and Angie finally had to drive along with the table sticking out of the sunshine roof, with Clare following in her own car. The sale wasn't supposed to start until ten but there were

already a lot of stalls at the site, and crowds of pro-
spective buyers walking round. The snow had cleared
and it was a bright but windy day. Someone directed
them to their allotted pitch and they pulled out some
boxes of goods so that they could get at the table, but
even before they had erected it a crowd of people created
a mêlée round, wanting to know what they had to sell.
One woman reached into a box and pulled out a very
nice stationery set with a good pen, looked it over and
said, 'How much for this?'

'It's marked,' Clare told her, struggling with the legs
of the table.

'I'll give you a pound.'

'It's priced at five.'

'You don't expect to get what you ask. Here's a
pound.'

The woman went to shove a coin into Clare's hand
but she grabbed the stationery set back. 'Sorry. No.'

'Suit yourself.' The woman gave her a nasty look and,
raising her voice so that everyone could hear, said, 'This
lot's over-priced. Not worth looking at.'

But the crowd wasn't put off and kept pulling things
out of the boxes before the girls could unpack them.
Some things they sold, but both of them gave a sigh of
relief when another car pulled up next to them and the
crowd pounced on that in turn.

'Good grief!' Angie gave Clare a horrified look. 'Is
it always like this?' Grimly they laid out their goods,
not even bothering with the cloth, and were devastated
to find that at least three things had been stolen during
the rush.

'I've made a terrible mistake,' Angie declared. 'I can't
do this.'

'You won't have to again,' Clare pointed out. 'This
is only a once-off; the antiques fairs will be much better,

you'll see. Come on, let's just forget about it and try
and sell the rest.'

Surprisingly, once they got the hang of it they started
to enjoy themselves, no longer minding when people
haggled with them because that was evidently part of
the buyers' fun. The people had come to get a bargain
and were satisfied if they could knock down the price a
little. Taking it in turns, the girls went round the rest of
the stalls, watching, listening, learning a lot. It was soon
obvious that there were people who must go to every
sale, both sellers and buyers, the sellers making a living
at it, the buyers on the look out for antiques and collectors' items, anything they could sell on again.

'Maybe this is where the antiques dealers buy their
stuff,' Angie suggested. 'Not that I'd fancy spending all
my time going around car-boot sales in the hope of
finding something.'

'No, much better to go to auctions.' Clare paused to
serve a customer, knocking a little off the price they'd
asked and giving a big smile, which sent the man away
happy. They had quite a few male customers, she found;
being two good-looking girls helped a lot. But they also
sold their things because they were all of good quality;
they had decided not to bring a lot of things that other
stalls were happily selling, like clothes and even shoes.
Some of their goods they'd priced too high, others too
low, and quite a few of the latter were bought by other
stall-holders to sell on.

'What a cheek!' Angie declared when this was done
by a man only a few cars down from them.

'Never mind. Look, these magazines aren't selling.
Let's take the prices off and sell them for what we can
get.'

There was a brief lull at lunchtime, giving them an
opportunity to have the coffee and sandwiches they'd

brought with them, but by two-thirty they had sold nearly everything they'd brought. Looking at her watch, Clare said, 'Angie, would you mind if I went now? Only Boyd's company are giving a cocktail party tonight and he especially wants me to go.'

'Of course not. You should have said. We may as well pack up anyway; I shouldn't think we'll sell much more.'

But the man from the stall further down the line who'd bought cheaply from them and sold the things on saw that they were packing up and came to try and haggle for what they had left, trying to push them into almost giving the things away. They finally got rid of him and loaded the table into Angie's car, and when Clare ran to get into her own car she found that it was boxed in, and it took her ages to find the owners of the other vehicles so that she could get out. She made good time when she eventually managed to leave, but it was almost four when she pulled into the drive and ran into the house.

Boyd was changed and ready to go, pacing impatiently up and down the room. 'I thought you said you'd try and get away early!' he exclaimed angrily.

Not bothering to explain, Clare ran upstairs to shower and change, but saw with horror that the wind had completely ruined her hair, which she'd set into a sleek style the night before. She could always wash it and just leave it to dry, of course, but somehow she didn't think the directors would go for a windswept Botticelli look. So instead she pulled it tightly back off her head and coiled it at the nape of her neck. Hatefully old-fashioned but all she could manage in the time. As it was, Boyd was out in the car with the engine running when she finally ran to join him.

As he pulled out into the road he said, 'Let's just hope we have a clear run—then we just might make it before the guests start arriving.'

Clare immediately turned on him. 'Don't you dare blame me for being late; you should be thanking me for getting here in time to go with you.'

'OK. Thanks for leaving your madly exciting car-boot sale to come and give me your support.' There was no gratitude in his tone, only sarcasm, but at least he'd said it.

Slightly mollified, Clare said by way of excuse, 'I would have been here over half an hour earlier if my car hadn't got boxed in.'

'If you knew that you were going to leave early it might just have occurred to you to leave the car where it *couldn't* get boxed in,' Boyd said acidly.

She gave him an angry glare, said, 'Men!' in a tone that women had been using for a thousand years, and sat back in her seat, refusing to speak to him for the rest of the journey.

Boyd drove like a Grand Prix driver that afternoon and they were doing really well until they reached the outskirts of London and were held up by a street market. He cursed, but there was nothing they could do except sit in the queue of traffic as it slowly crept along. They reached the hotel where the cocktail party was being held with about a minute to spare, and received a rather patronising, 'Thought you weren't going to make it,' from the managing director.

'Traffic problems,' Boyd said shortly, and took Clare's hand as they went forward to greet the first of the guests.

As it turned out, the party went off very succesfully. Clare had a drink and, despite their rush to get there, soon felt confident and relaxed. Now that she was coming here on her own terms the party didn't seem such a bind; she had done what she wanted that day and was willing to give the rest of it to Boyd's interests and to do her best for him. At one point he came over to give her a fresh drink and, leaning close to her, said, 'I like your hair like that.'

She glanced up and found his eyes smiling at her, sending messages that were as familiar and easy to read as if he had spoken them aloud. 'Thank you,' she said demurely.

'You're doing fantastically well.'

She smiled, but instead of thanking him again said calmly, 'I know.'

After the cocktail party things were fine between them again. During the next week Clare sent off the money she'd made at the car-boot sale to Mrs Prizbilski, following the clothes that she'd already sent. She also took samples of her work to several publishers of children's books, and it was received favourably, but she didn't get any definite commissions, although that was to be expected. And she took a day off to go to an auction, where Angie bought quite a lot of china to sell on, and Clare couldn't resist a couple of pieces for herself. They took the boxes of china back to Angie's, carefully washed it, and had great fun trying to date and ascribe each piece to a pottery. And, rather belatedly and certainly very reluctantly, Clare made a date to meet Melanie Stafford for lunch.

'Peter told me you were a great hit at the cocktail party,' Melanie said enviously.

'It's a shame you couldn't go.'

'One of the kids had a sore throat.'

Clare looked at her. 'Really?'

Slowly Melanie shook her head. 'I just couldn't face it.'

'You'll have to go some time.'

'I know, but I figure the longer I put it off, the more time there'll be for the managing director's wife to forget what I said.'

'If you leave it too long, they'll start wondering about you,' Clare warned. 'You might as well get it over and done with.'

'Yes, I suppose so,' Melanie sighed. 'I'll go to the next cocktail party, then. At least you'll be there to rescue me again.'

'No, I'm afraid I won't. I shan't be there. I'm going away for the weekend.'

Melanie stared. 'Isn't Boyd going either?'

'Oh, yes, he'll be there.' Clare said on a note of unconscious irony.

'But—doesn't he mind you not going?'

'Of course not,' Clare lied loyally. 'I have my own interests, you know.'

'Who's going to act as hostess, then?'

'I have no idea. One of the other director's wives, I suppose.'

'I shan't go,' Melanie said on a definite, frightened note. 'Not if you're not going to be there.'

'You'll be OK,' Clare encouraged. 'Just make sure you don't discuss any aspect of Peter's job with *anyone*. Be pleasant and polite, that's all.' She had been going to say be yourself, but changed her mind when she remembered how trusting Melanie was. 'Just keep your head down until you feel more confident.' She opened her bag. 'Look, I got these addresses for you. They are colleges that do courses called "How to enjoy being a company wife". You can take a one-day course or a five-session course, whichever suits you best.'

Melanie's eyebrows shot up. 'You mean, you can actually *learn* how to do it?'

Clare smiled. 'Yes, it seems there are a whole lot of women who are having exactly the same problems that you are. And if you can master the technique maybe you won't feel that it's such a subservient, superficial role.'

'Is that how you feel?'

After hesitating a moment, Clare nodded. 'Yes, I'm afraid I do. I also feel that you're used as a pawn, not only to help your husband, but also to anchor him to the job he's in because you'll feel obligated to the company for giving you such luxurious days out. You're more likely to discourage him from leaving if you feel you owe them something.'

'I hadn't thought of that,' Melanie admitted.

'You'll learn.' Clare touched her hand. 'Try not to be afraid. When it comes down to it they're just people, the same as you and Peter. And one day you might be in their position, summing up some new wife.'

'Well, I'll definitely make certain that she isn't afraid of me,' Melanie said forcefully. She smiled at Clare. 'Thanks, you've been a great help.'

'And will you go to the next cocktail party?'

But, 'I'll think about it,' the younger girl said cautiously.

It was cold on the Saturday morning when Clare and Angie set out for their weekend seminar, but they were full of high spirits, discussing their purchases and Angie's plans, wondering what the next two days would be like.

There were about thirty people assembled for the course. They met them in the lounge for coffee and found quite a lot of married couples, but among the singles there was actually a preponderance of men. Perhaps the next thing they noticed was that they were among the youngest there, only one married couple being about their own age. Also lots of the people already knew one another as this was a twice-yearly event which most of them had been going to for years. The organisers made them very welcome, introduced them to several people, whose first question was, 'What do you collect?' and lost interest when the girls said, 'Blue and white in general; we don't specialise.'

A great deal was packed into the first day: talks on patterns, commemorative china, tureens and their knobs—and that was all before lunch! After it there were more talks and then people were invited to bring up pieces they were unable to idenfify for the experts to look at. There were four experts, two women and two men, who took it in turns to give their opinion. Angie had put Clare's painting of her bowl on the table with the other pieces. One of the men, a Frenchman, picked it up and asked whose it was. When Angie put up her hand, he asked, 'Did you paint this?'

She shook her head and indicated Clare, sitting beside her. 'No, my friend did it for me.'

The Frenchman's eyes moved to Clare but then he turned back to the painting and talked about the pattern, placing it unerringly. He was really good, although they all were, making Angie and Clare feel very ignorant.

'I've got so much to learn,' Angie said with a wail when they went up to their room to change for the evening's dinner dance.

'Well, that's what we've come here for,' Clare pointed out.

'Yes, but I've learned so much already that I don't think my brain will take any more.'

The dance was for all the residents of the hotel, but their group tended to stay together. The girls sat at a table with the young couple and four other people who were on their own. They were asked to dance a couple of times and then the Frenchman came over and asked Clare to dance. His name, she recalled, was Luc

Chamond, and he was due to give a talk the following day.

'I admired your painting,' he said as they began to dance. 'Is it your hobby?' He spoke excellent English but had a deepish voice and enough accent for it to be attractive.

'No, I'm a commercial artist,' she told him.

His interest immediately deepened. 'Tell me about your work.'

Clare gave him a rough outline, but that wasn't enough; he wanted to know in detail, and she was still telling him when the dance ended. She thanked him and went to move away, but he put a hand under her elbow and led her out to the bar, where it was quieter. They sat down and he ordered a bottle of wine from the waiter without asking her what she would like. 'Go on,' he prompted.

'There really isn't much more to tell. I've recently worked up a new portfolio, which I'm taking round to publishers in the hope of getting some book illustrations to do.'

'You don't do your own work—pictures to please yourself, I mean?'

'Of course. When I have the time.'

Luc sat back and looked at her assessingly, then said, as if he was making a decision, 'I should like to see your work.'

Clare didn't quite know what to answer to that, so smiled a little and said, 'Thank you.'

'I mean it.' He took a card from his pocket and handed it to her. It gave his name, and his business address at an art gallery in Paris.

Clare stared. 'You work at an art gallery?'

'I also own it.'

She gulped. 'And you really want to see some of my work?'

He smiled, the thin-lipped, quizzical smile that only a Frenchman could carry off. 'I really do.'

Once, when she was young and single, Clare had been ambitious to become what she thought of as a serious artist, one who lived by selling her own original paintings, not just commissioned pictures, but that had been a dream that had dwindled away under the need to earn a living. But it hadn't completely died; perhaps it never would in any artist. But no art dealer had ever asked to look at her work before. He hadn't seen any yet, of course, and might immediately lose interest if he did, but at least he had asked! She looked at him more closely, noting the quiet but definite air of prosperity in his well-cut clothes and gold watch. He was middle-aged, his hair greying at the temples, but was still slim and athletic. Clare could imagine his swimming forty lengths every morning to keep fit. And he was unmistakably French. She couldn't define it exactly, but it was something in his face, its angularity and the shape of his jaw, and those thin lips, of course.

For a brief moment she wondered if this was the prelude to a pass. To test him she said, 'I have several paintings at home. If you would really like to see them perhaps you would care to come and have lunch one weekend? I'm sure my husband would be interested to meet you.'

His pale blue eyes crinkled a little, but he said gravely, 'I would very much like to see your work—and to meet your husband, of course.' He took a small leather diary with a gold pencil from his pocket. 'Shall we arrange a date?'

They finished their glasses of wine and Clare excused herself to go back to Angie. Luc stood up politely, making no effort to detain her and didn't ask her to dance again, merely nodding goodnight at the end of the evening.

When Clare got in bed that night she felt tired but unable to sleep. Was she, by the purest chance, to have a whole new world opened up for her? To have her work sought after instead of having to hawk it around? She felt full of excitement, even though she kept telling herself that Luc Chamond had only seen one example of her work and that he would probably hate everything else. But if there was a chance then she was determined to grab it with both hands and let *nothing* stand in her way!

CHAPTER SIX

LUC CHAMOND had said he would be in England again in three weeks' time. When Clare returned from the seminar she looked through her work and decided that it was all terrible, hopeless, and that he would never be interested in it. She felt like throwing all the paintings away and telling him not to bother to come. But so long as there was a chance... Her natural optimism reasserting itself, Clare realised that she needed more paintings to show Luc and decided to work up the sketches she had made in the snow.

Boyd had already left for a sales meeting in Milan when she got home from the seminar, and she didn't see him again until three days later. He came home quite early in the evening and found her in her studio, standing in front of an easel, and painting with absorbed concentration. She knew he was there but merely raised her free hand in acknowledgement, the tip of her tongue caught between her teeth as she painted in the delicate, trailing fall of a branch weighed down by snow. Boyd stayed in the room, a couple of yards behind her and out of her vision, knowing she didn't like anyone watching her while she worked. At last Clare straightened up, took a long, critical look at the painting and gave a small sigh of satisfaction.

'It's good,' Boyd said, coming up to slip his arm round her waist. 'One of your best.'

'Do you really think so?' She turned a glowing face up to receive his kiss.

'Haven't I just said so?'

115

'But it's important.' Putting her brush down, she turned and put her arms round his neck. 'I met someone who wants to see my work. He's a gallery-owner.'

Boyd's eyebrows rose. 'Really? Where did you meet him?'

'At the blue and white seminar. He's a collector, too. An expert. He saw the painting I did of Angie's bowl and said he would be interested to see more of my work.'

'On the strength of just one painting?'

Recognising the note of scepticism in his voice, Clare immediately became on the defensive. 'Not just that; he asked me about all my work.'

'You're sure it was your *work* he was interested in?' Boyd said sardonically.

She pushed him angrily away. 'You have a nasty mind, Boyd. Of course I'm sure.'

'How?'

'Because he's quite old, and because when I invited him here to see my work and to meet *you* he was quite agreeable. Honestly, Boyd, you ought to have more faith in my judgement by now. I'm not a teenager to be taken in by some man with a smooth line.'

Her cheeks were flushed, her eyes sparking with annoyance. 'OK. OK,' Boyd said soothingly. 'But just exactly what is he offering you?'

'Nothing. At least, nothing yet. He just said he would like to see my work. That's why I'm trying to get some more pictures finished.'

'You think he might offer to exhibit them?' Boyd kept his tone neutral.

'Oh, no, nothing so grand. But he might offer to take one or two to try and sell. I couldn't hope for more than that.'

Boyd nodded and put a hand on her shoulder. 'Don't get your hopes up too high, darling,' he said warningly.

'No, I won't.' But there was still an excited note in her voice that he recognised.

'Finished painting for today?'

'Yes. Sorry, I expect you're hungry. I'll just clean out my brushes and——'

'Why don't we eat out tonight?' Boyd suggested. He turned towards the door. 'I'm going to take a leisurely bath and change.'

'OK, fine.' Clare went to pick up the brush she'd been using but became aware that Boyd was standing by the door, waiting. 'Yes?'

'I just thought you might be interested in how the cocktail party went.'

Clare had completely forgotten about it, but the sardonic note in his voice brought back her guilt feelings and immediately antagonised her. 'I imagine they coped perfectly well without me,' she said stiffly.

'If by "they" you mean the organisers then yes, they did.' Boyd paused deliberately. 'But I have an idea that Melanie Stafford will never go to another company function.'

Clare looked at him in alarm. 'Why, what happened?'

'The managing director's wife acted as hostess in your place. She was wearing a very expensive-looking cream silk suit.'

'Oh, no!' Clare exclaimed in horror. 'Melanie didn't...?'

'She certainly did. She had some dark red drink full of fruit, and the whole lot went down the front of the woman's outfit—and a few pieces of fruit and ice got caught in her cleavage.'

'Ice as well?'

'Yes.' Boyd was unable to suppress a huge grin. 'You should have seen her wriggle and try not to gasp as it melted and went down.'

Clare tried to keep on looking horrified but couldn't, and they both burst out laughing. 'Oh, I *wish* I'd seen it. The managing director's wife takes herself so seriously. What did she *do*?'

'I had to hand it to her. Everyone in the room was staring at her, waiting for her to blow her top, but she handled it with great dignity; her face became a frozen mask and she just excused herself and went to her husband's office and stayed there.'

Clare's face sobered. 'What about Melanie?'

Boyd shook his head. 'She tried to apologise and wipe it off, but realised that she was only making things worse by dabbing at the stain. Then she saw the look on the woman's face. I'm afraid Melanie just burst into tears. She ran out of the room and Peter went after her. I went to see if I could do anything but she was having violent hysterics in the corridor, so I thought I'd better leave Peter to deal with it.'

'Oh, dear, poor Melanie. I feel partly to blame; she didn't intend to go but I persuaded her that she would be all right even though I wasn't going to be there.'

'It wasn't your fault; Melanie was just so nervous that she was shaking like a jellyfish.'

'She probably wouldn't have been so nervous if I'd been at the party,' Clare said regretfully.

'If you'd been there it wouldn't have happened anyway because the managing director's wife probably wouldn't have bothered to come.' Boyd gave an impatient shrug. 'What's the use of talking about what might have been? It happened.'

'How's Melanie now?'

'I don't know. I haven't been into the office since, and although I've spoken to Peter on the phone I thought it better not to mention it.'

'I think you're right; Peter seems to have a low patience threshold when it comes to Melanie's lack of social sophistication.'

Boyd gave her a swift glance. 'Is there likely to be trouble between them because of it?'

His question made Clare feel trapped. She wanted to be open with Boyd but Melanie had spoken to her in confidence, and Clare certainly didn't want to create more problems for the other girl. So she merely shrugged and said, 'How should I know? Even if there was, I'm quite sure Peter wouldn't let anything interfere with his work. He's like you,' she said with some irony, 'his career comes first.'

His face hardening, Boyd said curtly, 'That isn't true and you know it.'

Clare looked at him for a long moment, then came over and put her hands on his shoulders, looking intently up into his face. 'Sometimes I wonder.'

'Then you shouldn't.' Clare hoped he would enlarge on that but instead he pulled her to him and kissed her, then gave a groan as he looked at his jacket. 'I've got paint on my suit. You'd think I'd have learnt by now not to get amorous when you're in your working clothes.'

She laughed. 'Give me your jacket and I'll clean it off.'

He handed it to her, then said, 'I think I have some on my trousers.'

'Really? I didn't see any. Boyd!' She gave an exclamation as he kicked off his shoes and his trousers and then started unbuttoning his shirt. 'No! Not in here.' She ducked past him out of the door and began to run through the house, but he caught her at the bottom of the stairs. 'Boyd!'

But her protests were lost under his increasingly passionate kisses, under his hands as he stripped off her

clothes and caressed her, under his lips as they left her
mouth and sought the soft, intimate places, under the
primitive demands of his body as he took her in a blaze
of hungry sexuality. There was perspiration on her skin
and her hair clung to her forehead when Boyd finally
picked Clare up and carried her upstairs. He laid her on
the bed and grinned down at her, his hand casually
stroking the slimness of her waist. 'Did I hear you say
no?'

She gave him a satiated smile. 'You should see me
when I say yes.'

'How about tonight?'

'Certainly not!' She put on a mock-priggish face. 'You
can have too much of a good thing, you know.'

'No, I can't—not when the good thing is as luscious
as you,' Boyd said with certainty.

Clare laughed but was secretly pleased. Even though
they had been married for seven years and she was used
to Boyd's virility, he could still sometimes take her by
surprise, not only by his physical urgency, but also by
the steadfastness of his love for her. It had never once
wavered in all the years they had known one another,
not even when she had been so depressed after she'd lost
one baby after another.

Pushing that thought aside, as she always did, forcing
herself not to think about the past, she quickly sat up
and said, 'I'll get changed. Where shall we go?'

'Do you mind if we just walk up to the pub? I've had
enough of high living in hotel restaurants for a while.'

Clare's mental picture of what she had been going to
wear did a swift change, but she made no complaint,
knowing that he liked to relax and unwind after he'd
been away. 'OK. I'll be half an hour.'

'And you can tell me all about your weekend while
we're having dinner,' Boyd remarked.

The way he said it made Clare feel like some school-girl who had to account for every movement. She opened her mouth to protest but then shut it again. Boyd hadn't meant it like that; he was interested, that was all. It was natural that he should want to hear all about the seminar; after all, she didn't go away alone that often. Hardly ever, really, except occasionally to visit her mother.

As she stood in the shower Clare told herself off. I'm becoming obsessional about living my own life, she mused. But I've got to remember that I'm married. How can anyone who's married ever really live his or her own life? The very fact that you're willing to get married in the first place means that you've committed yourself to always being with someone else, and living the rest of your life as half of a couple, doing everything together, sharing everything. Although the sharing could be pretty one-sided sometimes; the thought came unbidden as her sense of injustice reasserted itself. But she pushed it aside again, adding it to the list of things it was best not to think about.

The next morning, after Boyd had left for the office, Clare received a letter from one of the children's book publishers that she'd visited, asking her to submit four preliminary sketches for a story that they'd enclosed. They wanted the sketches, of course, as soon as possible. And later in the morning one of the greetings-card manufacturers that she worked for rang to ask her to do twenty more paintings for them on a countryside theme. All of which was marvellous, but not when she was trying to finish the pictures she wanted to show Luc.

Clare worked really hard that day, going without lunch to try to get a picture finished, and was eagerly looking forward to telling Boyd her good news. But when he came home the first thing he did was to produce a list of dates for her diary. A picnic at Henley, lunch at the

Chelsea Flower Show, seats for Wimbledon, the conference at Bruges, three formal dinners, a day at the races, and two garden parties, as well as the next cocktail party. Clare read the list and didn't attempt to hide her dismay.

'I've tried to get you the full list so that you'll have as much notice as possible,' Boyd told her.

'So that I'll have no chance to make my own arrangements on any of those dates, you mean,' she said shortly.

'Those were your terms, if you remember—plenty of notice so that things wouldn't clash,' Boyd said imperturbably.

It wasn't what she'd meant at all, as he very well knew. 'We're hardly going to have a weekend to ourselves the whole summer,' she said angrily. 'There are far more functions on this list than we had to go to last year.'

'I wasn't a director last year.'

'Why are some of these functions marked with an asterisk?' She pointed to the list.

Boyd glanced over her shoulder. 'Those are the ones where you are to act as hostess.'

'Oh, am I? I suppose it never occurred to whoever arranges these to ask me first.'

'No, they asked me instead, and I said that you would be delighted to do so.'

'Oh, thanks very much!' And she threw the sheet of paper down on the floor in angry frustration.

'If you've already got something else on for any of these dates then you don't have to go.'

'These are months ahead; how do I know what might come along by then?'

Putting on his most reasonable and patient voice, Boyd said, 'Well, you can hardly ask the firm not to go ahead with any of these, or refuse to go to them, just in case something else *might* come along, now, can you?'

Clare glared at him. 'There are times when I almost hate you.'

'I'm only trying to comply with the terms you laid down.'

'No, you're not; you're deliberately getting in first so that I won't have a chance to opt out.'

'Most women would——'

'Don't you *dare* tell me that most women would just love to go to all these functions. I am *not* most women. I am me! And I *resent* having to give up so much of my time to your rotten company.'

Boyd, knowing he had taken a sneaky advantage, had been very patient, but now his face hardened. 'What do you want me to do—make the ultimate sacrifice, give up the job just so that you don't have to go?'

Clare's chin came up. 'Yes, why not? There are plenty of other jobs. Jobs that would employ just you and not expect your wife to act as an unpaid accessory.'

Angry himself now, Boyd, at his most sarcastic, said, 'Is it so bad, then, being wined and dined at the best places, being invited to take part in all the most prestigious social events in the calendar? It must be *really* hard on you.'

He turned to go but Clare grabbed his arm. 'Can't you understand? Having to go and smile and be nice all the time, to be charming to complete strangers who can hardly speak your language, or who are so big-headed that they want to talk about nothing but themselves? To have to laugh when men make a pass at you or touch you, because they're customers and you mustn't offend them? It makes me feel like—like a prostitute. A prostitute who doesn't even get paid!'

Boyd was staring at her, his face frozen into chiselled lines of cold anger. 'That,' he said forcefully, 'is the most

ridiculous and over-exaggerated thing I have ever heard!'
And he strode out of the room.

It had been a very short row but they both knew it
was one of their worst. Clare went into her studio and
locked the door, but was so angry that she couldn't lose
herself in the painting she had been doing, and made a
mistake that ruined it. Furiously blaming Boyd, she put
a fresh canvas on the easel and began slapping paint on
to it with uncontrolled venom. About half an hour later
Boyd came and tried to open the door. When he found
it locked he rattled the handle and called, 'What about
dinner?'

'Go to hell!' Clare yelled back.

Boyd's fist hit the door panel angrily. 'For heaven's
sake, grow up!' She didn't answer, and presently she
heard the front door bang as Boyd went out. She listened for the car but he must have walked because there
was no sound of the engine. Which meant he must have
gone up to the pub. Clare threw her paintbrush at the
canvas and burst into tears of anger. Today had started
off so well and now she just wished it had never begun.
She made herself some soup and ate it in the kitchen.
Boyd would have a meal at the pub, but if he expected
her to meekly join him then he could think again.

It was rather unfortunate that Melanie Stafford chose
that evening to phone. 'Is it all right to talk?' she asked.

Rightly guessing what she meant, Clare said, 'Yes, it's
OK; Boyd isn't here.'

'Peter has gone over to his mother's. He always does
that when we have a row.' Melanie sighed. 'I suppose
you've heard what happened at the cocktail party? Peter
says I've ruined his career.'

'I only heard that you had the bad luck to spill a drink.'

'But didn't Boyd tell you? It went all over the managing director's wife. It was a beautiful suit, too. It was

terrible. I wanted to die! Peter says he'll have to look
for a new job, that he'll never get anywhere in that
company now.' She paused, then said on a wail, 'Oh,
dear, I suppose I shouldn't have told you that. I'm *never*
going to learn.'

'It's all right, you know you can trust me.'

'Peter said they'll probably never invite me to another
party. Not that I want to go,' Melanie added woefully.

'Then don't,' Clare answered shortly.

'Don't?' Melanie sounded taken aback. 'But the social
functions are part of the job.'

'Peter's job, not yours. As a matter of fact,' Clare
said deliberately, 'I think that the company has no right
to expect us to attend these functions if we don't want
to, and if we do go then we're doing them a favour, not
the other way round.'

'Really? I wish Peter thought that. He wants me to
write a letter of apology to the managing director's wife.
That's why I phoned you; to ask you what I ought to
say.'

'I thought you apologised at the time.'

'Well, yes, but no amount of apologies would com-
pensate for——'

'Rubbish!' Clare interrupted shortly. 'Did Peter tell
you that? It was only a suit, for heaven's sake. It wasn't
as if you did her a permanent injury. If Peter insists on
you writing to her, just say that you're sorry about the
accident—because that's all it was, Melanie—and offer
to pay for the suit to be cleaned. I really don't see that
you have to do more than that.'

'It's so good to talk to you, Clare; you make me feel
so much better. Peter has been terrible since it happened; he treats me like some clumsy, mindless fool. And
I'm not. At least, I'm not most of the time. It's just that
he's forever warning me what to do and what to say and

what not to do and not to say. He kept on at me for days before that party and I was so nervous that I just *knew* I would do something terrible.' She paused, then said on a note of horror, 'Do you think it was psychological? That I subconsciously did it on purpose?'

'I don't know. Possibly. Maybe it was an inner revolt against doing something that you hated.' Clare laughed. 'Well, at least you can use it as an excuse not to go to any more parties for a while. I don't suppose Peter will want to risk something like it happening again for a very long time.'

Melanie's voice grew sombre. 'He hasn't just gone to see his mother; he's moved back there. He's so disgusted with me that he says he can't bear to live with me.'

'You mean, he's walked out over something as petty as that?' Clare's voice was horrified.

'It wasn't petty to him. He said it was terribly important that I make a good impression and now I've ruined everything.' And Melanie began to cry.

'Oh, Mellie, I'm so sorry.' But, after a couple of minutes of growing anger as she listened to the other girl's sobs, Clare cut through them, saying forcefully, 'Melanie, listen to me. Has it occurred to you that Peter is being thoroughly selfish over this? All he's thinking about is himself and his career. Has he given a thought to the way you must be feeling? Has he given you any support at all? Any encouragement? He should be helping you to get over this, not be putting you down. Mellie, are you listening to me?'

'Yes. Yes, I'm listening,' Melanie said in a thick, broken voice. 'But Peter...'

'You're got to stand up for yourself. Tell him that if the company hears that he's left you just for a little thing like a spilled drink then that won't do his career much good either. Tell him that you'll go on one of those company wife courses and, if you feel like it, you will then do the company a favour by attending what functions *you* want to attend. So long as it's convenient to you.'

'But I can't do that!'

'Yes, you can. Mellie, you have the advantage of Peter being at the beginning of his career. If you lay down your rules now he will have to accept them.'

'But if I'm successful at the course he'll want me to go to everything.'

'Refuse. Tell him that as the children grow older and you have more time then perhaps you'll feel able to go to more functions, but that the children come first. And make sure he accepts your terms; get it clear between you. Don't whatever you do let your life be governed by the company.'

Melanie was quiet and thoughtful for a while before she said, 'You sound as if you feel deeply about it.'

'Yes, I do,' Clare admitted. 'I have reason to. I let myself get caught up in all this and I'm finding it hard to try and change things.'

'I'll—I'll think about it,' Melanie promised.

'Don't just think—do it,' Clare insisted.

But when she put the phone down she wasn't at all sure that Melanie would have the strength of purpose to force the issue.

When Boyd came home later that night Clare was already in bed, the light out. Boyd undressed in the bathroom and slid quietly into bed, but he had only lain in silence for a few minutes before he reached out and took her arm. 'I know you're not asleep.'

But Clare didn't answer, tugging her arm away and turning to lie with her back to him. Boyd gave a snort of derision but didn't push it, and presently Clare heard the even tone of his breathing as he fell asleep. But she couldn't sleep, instead lying awake in the darkness, feeling herself a prisoner of her marriage. What should have been an equal partnership was becoming a cage.

There was an uneasy kind of truce between them next day and at the weekend they went to stay with Clare's mother because it was her fiftieth birthday and she was having a big party. Both Clare and Boyd were kept busy helping with the preparations, Clare with the food and Boyd organising the drinks. It was a good party, with her brother, Derek, and his family there as well as all her mother's many friends and neighbours. Derek's wife, Christina, helped to serve the food at the buffet table but after a while said, 'I'd better go and check on the boys; they often don't sleep well in a strange place.'

But she was soon back with a relieved smile on her face. 'They're OK.' Picking up her drink, Christina said, 'It's so nice to get away for a weekend occasionally, even with the boys.'

'You mean that you'd like to go away without them sometimes?'

Christina nodded. 'That would be heaven. I love them dearly, of course, but I long to be just a wife again instead of a mother, if only for a couple of days.' She looked at Clare, seemed about to say something, then hesitated and gave a slight shake of her head.

'What were you going to say?' Clare encouraged.

'Well... No, I couldn't possibly ask you—not in the circumstances.'

'Ask me what? Oh. You want me to look after the children for you.'

Christina looked uncomfortable. 'I'm sorry, for a moment I forgot about—that you can't have...'

'It's all right,' Clare said with a slight shrug. 'Yes, OK, we'll give it a try. I'll look after them for a couple of days for you and we'll see how it goes. You'll have to give me plenty of notice, though,' she said, remembering Boyd's list. 'My time isn't always my own.'

She wasn't aware that Boyd had come up to them, two tall glasses in his hands, until Christina turned to smile at him. 'Your champagne for the toast. Your mother is going to cut her cake now.'

'Oh, I must take a photograph!' Christina exclaimed, and hurried away.

Clare went to follow, but Boyd caught her arm, his eyes cold. 'Gossiping about our affairs?' he said harshly. 'Telling Christina your so-called problems?'

'No, as a matter of fact, I wasn't,' Clare retorted. 'But it just goes to prove that we do have problems if you won't even recognise them.' And she walked away from him to watch her mother cut her cake.

They were all awake till late that night, talking about the party and helping to clear up, and it was gone three in the monring before they got to bed. Clare used the bathroom first and was almost asleep when Boyd climbed in beside her and turned off the bedside light. She had her back turned towards him, as she had for the last two nights, but now he reached out for her and turned her over on to her back.

'I'm tired,' she protested.

'Then I'll wake you up.' And he began to kiss her neck.

'No, I don't feel like it.'

'Then I'll make you feel like it.' There was strong determination in his voice, an iron will that wasn't to be denied. His hand went to the straps of her nightdress and pushed them aside, and his lips found her breast. Clare put her hands on his shoulders to push him away but found herself gripping them instead. It had always been like this, she thought as his lips sent fiery sensations of desire shooting through her body. She had never been able to resist the sensuous need that he could always arouse in her. He came up on his knees to take her nightdress off completely, then switched on the light again and looked down at her, lying naked beneath him.

Almost idly he reached out to toy with her already rosy, tingling nipples, watching her reaction as his hands slowly moved down her body, stroking, caressing, finding the heart of her sensuality. Clare gasped and writhed under his skilful handling, her body aching for fulfilment, but still Boyd knelt over her. She moaned, arching her body towards him, and only then did he say, 'Do you want me? Do you?'

'Yes. Yes, you know I do.' There was a damp sheen of perspiration on her skin, but her voice was dry, hoarse with longing.

He lay down beside her. 'Take me, then.'

Clare opened her eyes and looked at him, read the demand for her surrender in his eyes. For an instant her mind rebelled, but the aching need he had awakened in her overwhelmed all other thoughts. Lifting herself up, Clare took his place, and he lay there as she lifted them both to frenzied, soaring heights of physical rapture.

When they woke in the morning Boyd made love to her again, and after that it was impossible to go on being angry, so things were more or less back to normal between them. They spent the day putting the house to rights after the party, watching while Clare's mother opened all her presents, and taking the children for a walk in the afternoon. Would she mind looking after them? Clare wondered as she watched her nephews trying to fly a kite that their father had made for them. Would they reawaken the longing for children that she was trying so hard to suppress? Probably. It would be difficult not to; it wasn't yet buried very deep. But she couldn't go through the rest of her life avoiding children.

The normality between them lasted until Monday evening when Boyd came home from work. He came striding into the kitchen where Clare was preparing dinner, his face a thunder-cloud. 'What the hell have you been saying to Melanie Stafford?' he demanded furiously.

'Melanie?' For a moment Clare looked startled. 'I don't know what you...' Then, 'Oh!' as realisation dawned.

'Quite! Peter came into the office this morning complaining that you'd been feeding Melanie all sorts of feminist rubbish about supporting the company only when it suited her, and not at all if she didn't feel like it.'

'And that's feminist rubbish, is it?' Clare said dangerously.

'It is when he needs her support.'

'And did he tell you that he'd walked out on her just because of what happened at the cocktail party?'

Boyd's head came up. 'No, he didn't. But obviously Melanie told you.'

'The poor girl had to talk to someone.'

'You had no right to interfere,' Boyd said shortly. 'Especially when you know that I'm Peter's boss. He must sort out his own problems. As it is, he had a just grievance against you—and therefore against me.'

'Melanie asked me for help.'

'Then you should have had enough sense to keep out of it.'

'Oh, great!' Clare said sarcastically. 'When the poor girl comes to me for help I have to turn round and say, "I can't talk to you, my husband wouldn't like it." What an enlightened, equal marriage we have!'

Boyd gave her an exasperated glare. 'The circumstances were such that——'

'Don't speak to me about the circumstances. I was happy to give Melanie some advice in the hope that it might prevent her from making the mistake I made in allowing myself to become just a company wife!'

Boyd's face set into a grim mask. '*Never*,' he said forcefully, 'interfere in anything or anyone to do with the company again.'

Furious at the implied challenge, Clare's head came up. 'Or what?' she demanded contemptuously.

His eyes glinted at her furiously. 'Don't push it, Clare.' And he strode out of the room.

They hardly spoke to each other over dinner and immediately afterwards Clare went back into her studio, firmly shutting the door. But she couldn't work; she was too uptight. Instead she turned off the light and went over to the deep window-seat, moved books out of the way to make enough room, and sat on it, her back against the wall, looking out into the moonlit garden. They were, she realised, fast reaching a crisis in their lives. Their marriage that had begun with such love and promise had somehow begun to fall apart. And Clare was very much afraid that it was all her fault. I've changed, she thought. In everything. No, not quite everything. She still loved Boyd and always would, but she was very much afraid that she could no longer live the life that he wanted.

But surely there must be some kind of compromise that they could reach. The last seven years couldn't just be thrown away; there had been too much love and joy for that. Although there had been sadness, too, when she had lost the babies, but the sadness had been mostly hers.

So what would it take for her marriage to be happy again? Clare mused. The answer to that was easy; just be the kind of wife that Boyd wanted—that he had married. Clare's mind immediately rebelled. I'm not that kind of person any more, and I don't want to be. But if she couldn't compromise and Boyd wouldn't change— what then? Clare shivered, afraid to look into the future.

At ten Boyd came into the room and found her still sitting by the window. He didn't knock, but paused when he saw that she was in the dark. Without turning on the light, he came over to her and handed her a mug of coffee, then sat on the other end of the seat.

'How's the painting going?' he asked.

Accepting the question as a kind of truce, Clare said, 'All right. I think I'll have enough to show Luc when he comes down.'

'That's the weekend after next, isn't it?'

'Yes.' Clare said it casually, but then her voice hardened. 'You don't have to worry, it won't interfere with the company's cocktail party on the Saturday; I invited Luc to come for Sunday lunch.'

'I know. I didn't say it for that.' Boyd's voice became rueful. 'I was trying to show you that I'm interested in your work and that I hope something comes of his visit, but you didn't take it that way.'

'I'm hardly likely to, am I?' Clare retorted.

Boyd was sitting on the shadowed half of the seat and she couldn't see his face clearly, but she heard him sigh deeply. For a few moments they sat in silence, but then Clare burst out, 'What's happening to us? Why are we so hateful to one another?'

Immediately Boyd set down his mug and came to put his arms round her, holding her as he stood beside her. 'Don't worry,' he said urgently. 'It's just a phase we're

going through. It will pass. So long as we go on loving
each other nothing else matters.'

But it does, Clare thought desperately. But even so
she put her arms round his waist and clung to him,
grateful for his physical closeness even if mentally they
seemed to be stretching further and further apart.

Two days before he was due to come and see her
paintings Luc Chamond telephoned to say that he was
sorry but he couldn't make the Sunday, and would it be
convenient for him to come on the Saturday evening
instead?

Clare, mentally cursing, afraid of losing this golden
opportunity, had to say that unfortunately she had to
go to a party being given by her husband's company
that evening. 'I'm terribly sorry, but I just can't get out
of it,' she explained.

'Of course not. I understand.'

'Perhaps the next time you come over?' Clare said
tentatively, thinking bitterly of all the hours of work she
had put in ready for this weekend.

'That might not be for some months. There is,
perhaps, one other possibility. I have a business meeting
on Monday morning, and I am due to fly back to Paris
in the afternoon, but if you could come up to London
and have lunch with me, and show me some of your
work, I could catch a later plane. If that is not too difficult for you?'

'Oh, no, it's not difficult at all. I can get to London
quite easily. Where shall I meet you?'

'I shall be at a friend's gallery.' He gave her the name
and address. 'Shall we say at twelve-thirty?'

'Yes. Fine. I'll see you on Monday, then.'

'I shall look forward to it. And, again, my apologies,
Clare.'

Clare expected Boyd to give her an 'I told you so' look when you told him that Luc Chamond couldn't make Sunday, but he merely said, 'That's unfortunate. Can't you make some other arrangement?'

'We have. I'm meeting him in London on Monday instead. He's giving me lunch.'

'Just you?' Boyd was unable to hide the slightly sardonic twist to his mouth.

Clare could have said a lot, but she kept a hold on her temper and said calmly, 'That's right—after all, I am the one he might be doing business with.'

'Yes—but I would have liked to meet him.'

'Look him over, you mean.'

Boyd gave one of his sudden, heart-stopping grins. 'Can't help being jealous of my gorgeous wife,' he told her.

How could you fight against that? Clare couldn't. And she ended up telling Boyd where she was meeting Luc.

'I'll drive you there,' he offered. 'Save you carrying your portfolio around London.'

'But if I drive up to London with you it will mean hanging around for hours, waiting.'

'Then we'll go up later.'

Clare tried to argue but he wouldn't listen, finding an answer to all her protests, then flooring her by saying, 'Why are you so against my meeting him?'

'I'm not. I just think that you ought to trust me.'

'I do. I just want to know if I can trust this Chamond guy.'

'Oh, for heaven's sake!' Clare exclaimed furiously.

But she lost the battle. Boyd insisted on driving her up to London and parked right outside the gallery.

'You're not allowed to park here,' Clare pointed out. 'There's a yellow line.'

'We'll take a chance. Here, I'll carry your portfolio for you.'

'I can manage.'

But he ignored her and carried it into the gallery, Clare following in scarcely controlled anger.

It was quiet inside after the busy street, the gallery warm and carpeted. There was an exhibition of animal paintings, mostly traditional, with a few modern pictures of cats at the far end. A very smart woman with a sleek hair-do and too much make-up was sitting at the reception desk. She looked to be in her mid-thirties, so was probably over forty. 'Can I help you?'

Clare drew herself up. 'I've an appointment with Luc Chamond. He arranged to meet me here.'

'Mrs Russell?'

'Yes.'

'One moment.'

The woman picked up an internal phone and waited for it to be answered. As she did so her eyes travelled over Boyd, quite frankly liking what they saw. Clare glanced at Boyd and saw amused acceptance of the woman's admiration in his eyes. She glared at him, thinking that he had deliberately accompanied her here so that he could check on Luc Chamond but was quite prepared to flirt himself.

'Monsieur Chamond will be with you in one moment,' the woman said after speaking into the phone.

Almost at once Luc emerged from a door at the end of the gallery and came towards her. 'Clare.' He shook her hand. 'It was kind of you to come all this way.' He glanced at Boyd.

'My husband,' Clare said shortly. Adding lamely, 'He carried my portfolio for me.'

The two men shook hands politely, each eyeing the other.

'Shall we take your work over to the table here?' Luc suggested. Taking the portfolio, he undid the tapes and looked at her paintings one by one, taking his time but making no comment. Clare stood nervously by, waiting, glad that Boyd had at least had the tact to stay out of earshot. He was talking to the woman at the desk, who was smiling up at him. Eventually Luc looked at the last picture and re-tied the tapes. Then he turned to Clare and said merely, 'Shall we go to lunch?'

Unable to read his reaction, Clare was still anxiously nervous as she gave the portfolio to Boyd and said shortly, 'See you tonight,' before walking through the door that Luc held open for her.

Boyd followed, saying, 'Perhaps I can drive you somewhere?' then broke off as he saw that a traffic warden was standing by the car, about to write out a parking ticket. But the warden was a woman, and he quickly went towards her with his disarming grin.

He would talk her out of giving him the ticket, Clare knew, but it would take time. Not bothering to wait, Luc held up an arm and a taxi drew up beside them almost at once. The two of them got in, and Clare hardly bothered to look at Boyd's face as they sailed by him.

They had ordered lunch in a small, comfortable restaurant, and were sipping their aperitifs before Luc even mentioned her paintings. A Frenchman getting his priorities right, Clare thought as she waited. Then he smiled and nodded. 'I like your work. You have talent. As I thought when I first saw your painting at the seminar, your eye for detail is extraordinary. And you have a style of your own that you should work on, develop.' He paused for a moment while Clare waited breathlessly for him to go on, but he said, 'Your husband; is he in favour of your paintings?'

It was a strange way to put it but Clare knew what he meant: was Boyd likely to make objections if Luc helped her? 'Yes,' she said without a qualm. 'He won't stand in my way.'

Luc looked into her earnest face and nodded, satisfied. 'Then I will help you to exhibit some of your paintings. But not in my main Paris gallery. I have an interest in a smaller gallery near Montmartre. I will arrange for you to share an exhibition there with another artist. Perhaps in April or May.'

Clare gazed at him in stunned joy, hardly able to speak until she realised that Luc was waiting for her to say something. 'But that's wonderful! Marvellous! Thank you so much. I'm so grateful.'

He nodded, pleased to be thanked so warmly. 'Maybe I will try to persuade my friend who has the gallery where we met today to take one or two of your paintings also,' he said with an expansive gesture of his hand.

Clare thanked him again and listened, fascinated, as he began to talk about famous painters he had known and even more famous paintings that he had shown in his galleries. He was a good talker, able to tell an anecdote to get the most out of it, making her laugh, making her long wistfully to be part of the world of artists. She hardly noticed what she ate and the time flew by, until, regretfully, the meal was over and Luc had to take a taxi to his hotel to collect his luggage and catch a plane at the City Airport.

On the pavement outside the restaurant he took her hand again and bowed over it in a gallant way that completely captivated her. 'It has been a great pleasure to talk with you,' he told her. 'I will telephone you about the exhibition very soon.'

'It's been a real pleasure for me, too,' Clare said warmly. 'Thank you for lunch—and for your interest.'

She watched as his taxi drew away, thinking how relaxed and pleasant the last couple of hours had been. Not only because they had talked about art, but also because there had been no tension, no competition, as there always seemed to be lately with Boyd. Probably because Luc was so much older, a comfortable father-figure who only wanted to help and encourage her in her chosen career instead of a demanding husband who wanted to rule her life. Clare sighed heavily, and turned reluctantly away.

CHAPTER SEVEN

AFTER Luc Chamond had left, Clare walked slowly along the street, wondering whether to go straight home or to go to Boyd's office first. In the end she did neither, going instead to the Wallace Collection, housed in a building off Oxford Street in the heart of the West End, to look at the pictures. It was one of her favourite places; less crowded than the Tate and the National Galleries, the surroundings more like a richly furnished house than a museum. Clare stayed there for an hour or so, her excitement at the possibility of her pictures being shown in an exhibition receding a little as she looked at the paintings by famous masters and realised that she would never be anywhere near as good. But she could learn, and she could go on trying.

At four-thirty Clare took a cab to Boyd's office building, her anger at the way he had behaved largely evaporated under the calming influence of the pictures. She had a leisurely chat with the doorman before taking the lift to Boyd's new floor. But only Velma the Vamp was there, looking sophisticated in a grey sweater and straight skirt with a rich, deep-pink-coloured silk scarf loosely knotted at her neck.

'I'm afraid Boyd is in a meeting,' Velma said, her hand going to the scarf.

'I'll wait in his office, then.' Clare walked in, dropped her bag on the settee and sat down, then turned as Velma followed her in.

'Can I get you a coffee or something?'

Surprised, Clare said, 'Thanks. A coffee would be nice.'

She expected Velma to go to a communal staff kitchen to make it, but Boyd's secretary walked familiarly over to what looked like a cupboard set into the panelling, and opened the door to reveal a shelf with a small sink and a plug-in kettle, and under it a fridge, for drinks presumably. One of Boyd's perks on becoming a director.

'Is it cold outside?' Velma asked conversationally as she waited for the kettle to boil. 'You look quite windswept.'

Taking that as a suspiciously catty remark rather than an innocuous observation, Clare said, 'Yes, it is cold and very windy.'

'It certainly feels chilly after Italy,' Velma said quickly. 'It was much warmer there.'

'Really?' Warning bells began to go off in Clare's brain.

'Yes, when I was in Milan with Boyd.' Velma poured out the coffee and brought it over. 'Boyd did tell you I was with him in Milan, didn't he?'

Clare smiled at her sweetly. 'He doesn't bother to tell me things that aren't of any importance.'

The secretary's face hardened, but then she touched the scarf again and said, 'Do you like this?'

'Very nice,' Clare said warily.

'Boyd bought it for me while we were there. He said he thought the colour suited me.'

'Puce?' Clare said in affected disbelief. 'Yes, well, Boyd is always polite to everyone.' And added quickly, 'Thanks for the coffee. Don't let me keep you; I'm sure you have some terribly important letters to type or bits of paper to file.' Leaning forward, she picked up a magazine from the coffee table and opened it, dismissing the other girl.

Faced with only the back of a magazine to make remarks at, Velma tossed her blonde head and strode out of the office, not quite slamming the door but near enough.

When she was safely out of the room Clare slowly lowered the magazine. It was far from being the first time that another woman had made a play for Boyd; he was much too good-looking not to attract them, but usually they hadn't been so open about it. But she had always known because Boyd had told her about them, if she hadn't already guessed. But Velma had been more than open; she'd pushed it down Clare's throat. And Boyd hadn't told her that he'd taken Velma with him to Milan. Which in itself was odd; he usually told her everything. Then Clare remembered that they hadn't been on exactly close terms the week before he went to Milan because he was annoyed that she'd insisted on going to the seminar with Angie instead of the company cocktail party. So maybe the fact that Velma had gone with him had just been overlooked. That must be it.

But it eased Clare's mind for only a moment. Velma had been too confident, too determined to let her know that she was attracted to Boyd for there not to be something behind it. Or maybe she was cleverer than Clare had thought and had taken this opportunity to make Clare jealous and suspicious, to push her perhaps into a fight with Boyd over something that didn't exist until the fight created it. And which might, whether Velma knew it or not, push an even bigger wedge between them, the way things stood at the moment. Thinking about it, remembering Boyd's continuing need for her, Clare had no real doubts that he had been unfaithful with Velma, although it was possible, of course, while they had been in Italy. He certainly wouldn't be the first married man to take advantage of a woman who threw herself at his head.

But Boyd wasn't like that. They loved each other and had no need to be unfaithful. Clare tried to push the thought out of her mind, but the nagging seed of doubt had been planted, as Velma had intended it should. And Velma, of course, had the advantage over the other women who had made a play for Boyd in the past in that she was with him for hours on end, for five days a week. And she also had an advantage that she probably didn't know about, because lately Boyd had been coming home from an adoring secretary to a less than welcoming wife.

Clare went to sip her coffee but then decided that she couldn't possibly drink anything that Velma had made, so got up and poured it down the sink. Looking through the fridge instead, she poured herself a gin and tonic and went to sit in Boyd's chair, leaning back and putting her booted feet up on his desk in an action of defiance. Her biggest weapon against Velma, she thought, was to say nothing to Boyd, to treat her disclosure with the contempt it deserved. But, Clare being human, that was going to be extremely difficult. There was always another, more certain way to make sure that Velma faded from the scene, of course. That was to become again the kind of wife that Boyd wanted. She could then insist that Velma be transferred to some other department, although it would hardly be necessary then because Boyd would have no temptation to stray.

An angry sound escaped from her and Clare banged her fist on the desk. Everything seemed to be conspiring against her lately. Was she to have no chance for any independence? But she'd be damned if she gave up trying just because of Velma the Vamp. If Boyd could be hooked by a woman as obvious as that then to hell with him! But she didn't want him to be hooked by Velma or anyone. He was hers and only hers, and she would do everything in her power to keep him. The thought came instinctively to her mind, pulling her up short, making her wonder what sacrifices she would be willing to make to keep Boyd—and whether she might have to make them.

She was still sitting pensively at the desk when Boyd walked in ten minutes later. Peter Stafford was with him and both men looked surprised to see her, so Velma obviously hadn't warned them she was here. If she had Boyd would most likely have got rid of Peter, knowing that he was angry with Clare for having such a straight talk with Melanie. As it was, Peter's face hardened and a malicious look came into his eyes when he saw the way she was sitting, with her feet still up on Boyd's desk and the glass in her hand.

Boyd's eyebrows rose a little and he gave her a wary look, expecting her at least to be angry with him, and afraid that Luc Chamond hadn't liked her work and that she was drowning her disappointment. So he was pleasantly surprised when she smiled at him and raised her glass. 'Hi. I'm celebrating.'

He walked round the desk. 'He liked them?'

'He liked them.'

'Congratulations, darling.' He leaned down to kiss her. 'Shall we go out tonight to celebrate together?'

'Of course.' He kissed her again, and then she looked round at Peter Stafford. 'Hello, Peter,' she said calmly.

'Clare,' he acknowledged stiffly. He opened his mouth to say something, hesitated as he glanced at Boyd, and then shut it again.

Rightly guessing that he would have had a go at her if Boyd hadn't been his boss, Clare shamelessly took advantage of the fact to say sweetly, 'How's Melanie—or haven't you seen her lately?'

Boyd put his hand on her shoulder and pressed hard, reminding her of their row and his unspoken threat.

'She's all right—but no thanks to you, Clare, I might add,' Peter said abrasively.

Swinging her legs down off the desk, Clare stood up. 'Might you? I suppose it rather depends on whether you want a happy, interesting girl or a submissive doormat for a wife, doesn't it?'

He could find nothing to say to that and Boyd said smoothly, 'We'll discuss the outcome of the meeting tomorrow, Peter. I expect you're anxious to get home.'

'Yes. Yes, of course. Goodnight.' He went out, closing the door behind him, but Clare was willing to bet he was having a go at her to Velma in the outer office.

'You are an incorrigible minx,' Boyd told her.

Clare wrinkled her nose at him, knowing how to charm. 'Would you have me any other way?'

Boyd grinned and put on a mock-American accent. 'I'll have you any way I can get you, honey.'

'You are so lewd!' She pretended to be angry and hit him in the chest with her fist.

He laughed and put his arms round his waist. 'What did your Frenchman say?'

'I'll tell you over dinner. My treat!'

'Wow! It can only be a promise to take over the entire National Gallery for an exhibition of your work.'

She hit him again.

'If we weren't in this office...' he threatened.

'You'd what?' Putting her arms round his neck, she pressed her hips against his, moving voluptuously, making him groan deep in his throat.

Having sat at his desk for so long, Clare had no difficulty when she reached her hand down in locating the

'Call' button on his console. Velma immediately walked
in without knocking and found them still close in each
other's arms. Boyd had his back to the door and wasn't
even aware that she had come in, but Clare looked at
her over Boyd's shoulder, then closed her eyes again as
she returned Boyd's kiss. The door slammed as Velma
went out and Boyd went to lift his head, but Clare put
her hand in his hair and held his mouth against her own.

That night was a really good one, not only in the restaurant but also later at home in bed, where Clare insisted that they take a bottle of champagne.

'You should have news like this more often,' Boyd
commented as he leaned back on the pillow.

Clare let some wine trickle down his chest and then
bent to lick it off. 'Being successful makes one happy.
You should know that.'

'Of course I do. But I wasn't aware that it could also
make *you* so sexy. Hey, that tickles,' he complained.

'Don't you like it?'

'Have I told you to stop?'

'Are you going to?'

'I may open another bottle.'

She laughed and poured some more, and a few minutes
later gave a great gasp as, unable to stand it any longer,
Boyd grabbed her and pulled her beneath him.

During the next few days Clare found it very hard not
to ask him outright about Velma going with him to
Milan, even though she knew it would be far wiser not
to mention it. But over dinner one evening he said that
he would be late home every night for a couple of weeks
as he had to go to a language laboratory to brush up his
French. 'That way I won't need to take an interpreter
with me when we go go Bruges.'

'Most people in Europe speak English as a second
language anyway, don't they?' Clare remarked.

'Yes, but they appreciate it if you make some attempt to speak their own language.'

Seeing a golden opportunity, Clare said, 'Who did you use as an interpreter in Italy?'

'In Milan? Oh, that was Velma, my secretary. She speaks fluent Italian.'

So that was it. Clare gave an inner sigh of relief. 'Velma the Vamp? I'm amazed.'

'She's quite clever, you know. She wouldn't have got the job if she hadn't been.'

'No, I suppose not,' Clare said thoughtfully. 'I suppose she's ambitious?'

'Of course. She's already making noises about being made my personal assistant.'

'And will you give her the job?'

Boyd shrugged. 'It would only really be a change of title. Her responsibilities wouldn't increase much.'

'But she could legitimately ask for a rise to go with the better-sounding title.'

'You've got it in one,' Boyd laughed. Reaching across the table, he took her hand. He had been happy the last few days because she had stopped work early to cook his dinner, had put his interests before her own, and generally made a fuss of him, especially in bed. Acting the good wife almost as she had done when they were newly married and he had been all that mattered, her entire world. Before time and familiarity had opened up her life to encompass other interests, other needs. Looking at him, Clare thought how selfish men were, how demanding, only completely happy if they had everything their own way. Well, they'd had it their own way for a couple of thousand years; now it was time to give the second sex a chance.

'What are you thinking?' he asked.

She blinked, then said coquettishly, 'Wouldn't you like to know?'

'I hope it was about me.'

Her lips curled in amusement. 'Yes, in a way I suppose it was.'

'Would you like to come up and take the refresher course with me?'

Her heart warmed, but Clare shook her head. 'I've got too much work to do to travel up to London every day. And I want to finish some more pictures for Luc to choose from.'

'Have you heard from him yet?' Boyd asked, sitting back in his chair.

'No, but it's early days yet.'

Picking up his wine glass, Boyd looked at it reflectively for a moment before saying, 'I'd advise you to be very careful where Luc's concerned, darling.'

'Why? Do you think he's lying, that he hasn't got a gallery?'

'Oh, he owns the gallery all right. I checked.'

Clare stared at him. 'You checked up on him?'

'It's sound practice to check that people you intend to do business with are what they say they are. You must know that.'

'Yes—but I think you might have asked me first.'

'Why? You're sensible; you could only say yes, so what was the point of asking?'

Putting her hand underneath the table, Clare balled it into a tight fist, but kept her voice calm as she said, 'So you decided to check on his business reputation as you checked on him personally when you insisted on coming with me to the gallery. And what did you find out?'

'His business is sound. He acts as an art consultant as well as running his galleries in Paris and Monte Carlo.

And he does have an interest in a couple of smaller galleries as well.'

'So he's everything he said he was,' Clare said triumphantly. 'So why warn me to be careful?'

'Because he has quite a reputation where women are concerned. He's too smooth, Clare; surely you can see that?'

'Don't all Frenchmen have a reputation where women are concerned?' she said shortly. 'And, anyway, he's old; he must be over fifty.'

'You think his age makes any difference?' Boyd exclaimed. 'That's all the more reason for him to fancy young girls.'

'You can hardly call me that any more. I'm a woman, not a young girl.'

'You are to him. Just watch him, Clare.'

She rose angrily to her feet. 'It's my work he's interested in.'

Boyd, too, got to his feet and caught her wrist. 'There must be hundreds of talented artists in France that he can choose from.'

'But he likes *my* work.'

'And maybe he likes your work because you're female and young and beautiful. Don't forget the "casting couch" syndrome, Clare.'

'Oh, for heaven's sake!' She shook off his hand. 'You tarnish everything.'

'I'm only trying to warn you.'

She glared at him. 'Warn *me*! Huh, you're a fine one to talk.'

She swung away and went into the kitchen, but Boyd followed her. 'What's that supposed to mean?'

About to have a go at him about Velma, Clare suddenly saw that she was on the brink of doing what the other girl wanted. Gritting her teeth, she said, 'Just get off my back, Boyd.'

'That wasn't what you were going to say.'

'Well, it's what I'm saying now. You told me not to interfere in your business, but you don't even bother to ask before you interfere in mine.'

'I'm trying to help you.'

'Well, maybe I don't want your help. Maybe I'd like to have the privilege of making my own mistakes.'

'You're crazy,' Boyd said in disbelief. 'Who wants to make mistakes if they can avoid it?'

'Oh, you just can't see it, can you?' Clare said in angry frustration. She pulled on her rubber gloves and began to fill a bowl with hot water.

'What are you going to do?'

'Clean out the oven.'

'But it's clean; it doesn't need to be done.'

'But *I* need to do it. Look, why don't you go round the pub or something?'

He stared at her for a moment, then turned and went into the sitting-room, but he didn't go out. Clare attacked the oven until she was tired and then went straight up to have a bath. Usually she didn't lock the door when she had a bath, but now something made her reach out and push the bolt across.

When Boyd came up a short time later he rapped on the door and said, 'You OK, Clare?'

'Yes, fine. I'm having a bath.'

'I'll wash your back for you.' Boyd went to open the door but found it locked against him. 'Hey, you've forgotten to unbolt the door.'

'Oh. Have I? Never mind; I can manage.'

She stayed in the bath, reading, until the water grew cold, then put on her nightdress and dressing-gown before she tiptoed into their bedroom. Boyd had used the other bathroom and was already asleep. Clare gave a small sigh of relief and slipped between the sheets, turning off the bedside lamp. As she did so Boyd grunted and turned over towards her. His arm went over her, across her waist, possessive even in his sleep, because he didn't waken, though Clare was afraid he would and lay very still. This is silly, she scolded herself. But somehow she didn't want sex tonight; she was fed up with acting the dutiful wife, the harem girl, the doormat. And she certainly didn't want another fight; she was tired of those, too. I just can't win, she thought before she fell asleep.

The next day was Saturday and Boyd was booked to play in a tournament at the squash club, but Clare had promised to design some business cards and posters for Angie, who came round at eleven.

'I've worked on a few ideas,' Clare said as they went into her studio. 'Will you be having the cards printed?'

'No, unfortunately I can't afford that yet. It will have to be something I can get photocopied.'

'That's a shame, because a card with a little painting of a blue and white plate and your name and address would have looked good.'

She showed Angie the sample design, and the other girl gave an exclamation of pleasure. 'Hey, that's really eye-catching. Oh, I wish I could afford it. You've put such detail into it.' Angie lifted her head. 'Have you thought of going into the business-card design business?'

They looked at each other and both burst into laughter.

'Enterprise, that's the name of the game,' Angie declared.

'When are you going to have your first stall?'

'There's an antiques fair coming up at the beginning of April. That will give me time to go to one more auction to get enough stock to sell. That's if you can make it to come with me, of course.'

Clare looked at her with some misgivings. 'You don't expect me to come with you every time you have a stall, do you, Angie?'

'No, of course not, but I'd be grateful to have someone with me the first time.'

'I'll get the engagement diary.'

They looked up the date and Clare found that she and Boyd were due to go out to dinner with some friends in the evening but there was nothing booked during the day. 'That's a date, then,' she said, writing it in.

Angie's eyes sparkled. 'The day I start my own business.'

'And become your own boss instead of somebody else's wage slave.'

Angie lifted her coffee-mug in a toast. 'I'll be an entrepreneur.'

'I'll drink to that.' Clare clicked her mug against Angie's. 'Here's to your first million.'

'Million!' Angie gave a wry laugh. 'I'll be lucky if I make a profit. But it will be a hell of a lot better than office work. And to hell with Ian,' she added with forceful determination.

Clare's eyes widened. 'Dare I ask what that's supposed to mean?'

'I've decided to give up my job completely,' Angie said defiantly. 'I just can't stand it any longer. Ian, of course, is dead against it. He says why give up a steady income for one where I might not make any money at all? Using undeniable male logic, he says the whole idea is stupid. But I've been working in an office since the day I left school, Clare, and I'm sick of it. I've got to get out. OK, so I might not succeed and I'll have to go back to work, but at least I'll have tried.'

'Good for you,' Clare said warmly. 'But what about your idea of doing part-time work until you get established?'

'I've changed my mind about that. I think I should give my whole time and attention to this new career.'

'But wouldn't Ian be happier if you compromised?'

'I'm not in the mood for compromise. I looked to him to support me in this, but at first he thought it was just a joke, then, when he realised I was serious, he——' She broke off, her cheeks flushed, and it didn't take much guessing to realise the row that must have ensued. 'Well, if he doesn't like it he can do the other thing,' Angie said shortly. 'That's what I told him, and I mean it.'

'Think what you're doing, Angie,' Clare cautioned in alarm. 'Is it worth forcing the issue over a change of career?'

'It isn't just a change of career; it's my whole future. If I don't make a stand now I'm going to lose my chance forever.'

Clare inwardly agreed with her, but at the same time felt uneasy about the hornets' nest she had helped to create. Quickly she changed the subject back to the leaflets she had designed for Angie. 'Would you like me to stick the little painting on for you? It should come out all right in black and white.'

'Yes, please. Then I can run some off at work before I leave.'

'I should have some glue somewhere.' Clare looked on her work table but couldn't find it. 'Now I come to think of it, I seem to remember Boyd borrowed the glue last week. I'll see if it's on his desk. I'll only be a minute.'

She went out to the old bureau in the sitting-room that Boyd used as a desk, but couldn't find the glue in any of the pigeon-holes. Then she noticed his documents case on the floor beside it. Maybe the glue was in there. It was one of the modern cases with a code-numbered lock instead of a key. The code was a combination of their birthday dates and then the two added together, Clare remembered. She punched in the numbers, opened the case, and gave a grunt of satisfaction as she found the glue in one of the pockets. She was about to close the case when she noticed the corner of an envelope with a foreign stamp on it. The stamp looked familiar and she pulled out the envelope to have a closer look. She was right; it was a Polish stamp, and she recognised the handwiting as that of Mrs Prizbilski. What was Boyd doing with the letter she'd sent? But the envelope was much thicker and stiffer than Clare remembered. Frowning, she opened it and took out not only a letter but also a photograph. It was of two small babies dressed in identical clothes. Fair-haired, appealing.

For a moment Clare could only stare at the photograph, trying to work it out, then she quickly looked again at the envelope. It wasn't the original letter; this one was post-marked February, but addressed only to her, not to both of them. A flush of anger came to her cheeks as she opened the letter and deciphered Mrs Prizbilski's writing. It was on much the same lines as before, thanking Clare for the money and the clothes, and saying that the twins must soon be sent to an orphanage and perhaps parted for life unless someone adopted them before too long. Clare hardly took it in, she was too angry. Pushing the letter and photo back in the envelope, she put it in the bottom drawer of the bureau, under some old theatre programmes, then closed the case and went slowly back to the studio, bright spots of colour in her pale cheeks.

Angie had found the painting she had done in her fury a couple of weeks before and had propped it on the

window-sill so that she could stand back and look at it.
'I didn't know you did anything like this,' she said in
an uncertain voice, not sure whether she was supposed
to like it or not.

'No, that was—an exception.'

Something in Clare's tone made Angie swing round
to look at her. 'I'm sorry, shouldn't I have brought it
out?'

'What? Oh, no, it doesn't matter.' Clare sat down, her
mind still on the letter. Somehow she felt more betrayed
by Boyd's having hidden it then whan she'd found out
that he'd taken Velma with him to Milan without telling
her. Becoming aware that Angie was looking at her cu-
riously, she roused herself and said, 'I've got the glue.
Let's stick the picture on and see how it looks.'

Angie was happy with the result and Clare didn't encourage her to stay when she said she ought to go. After
seeing her friend off, Clare went back into the sitting-
room, read the letter from Poland again and took a
longer look at the photograph. It was just a snapshot,
not very well focused, but they looked sweet babies,
identical in looks, but one yawning, the other wide awake
and smiling. Would their temperaments be different,
then? Clare wondered. One active, the other a dreamer?

But she wasn't so concerned with the contents of the
letter as with Boyd's having hidden it away. From the
postmark, it must have arrived at least two weeks ago.
And he obviously had no intention of ever showing it
to her because too much time had gone by for her not
to query it. So why had he hidden it? Well, that was
obvious, too: because he didn't want her to get ideas
about adoption; of these children or any other. A flood
of bitter anger swept through her. Boyd had no right to
keep this from her, to make decisions for her. But now
she had a decision to make for herself, what to do about

the letter. Glancing at her watch, she saw that it was almost one. Boyd would be home any moment, hungry for his lunch. Taking the letter, Clare spread it out on the opened flap of the bureau, the snapshot beside it, where he couldn't help but see it. Then she put on her coat and went out for a walk.

Boyd's car was in the drive when she got back an hour or so later. The walk hadn't calmed her at all—instead she had worked herself up into a cold, and in her view perfectly justifiable, anger. She let herself in by the back door and hung up her coat in the little hall leading to the kitchen. Boyd was in the sitting-room; she could hear him moving around and he had the radio on. Clare hadn't eaten but it didn't occur to her to make herself a sandwich or something; instead she went straight into the sitting-room and turned off the radio.

Boyd was sitting at the table in the bow window, mending a hair-drier that had stopped working. He looked up when she walked in and his mouth twisted into a wry grin when he saw the anger in her face. Putting down the tools he was using, Boyd said, 'All right, you're spoiling for a fight, so we might as well get it over with.'

His half-exasperated tone added to her rage, but she kept her voice level as she said coldly, 'Perhaps you'd like to tell me why you found it necessary to conceal a letter that was addressed to me?'

'Because I didn't want you to see it,' he answered bluntly.

'Don't treat me like an idiot. Why did you hide it away?'

He got to his feet, hesitated for a fraction of a second, then said, 'Because the subject is a sensitive one. Because I didn't want you to be upset all over again. Because we'd made our decision after Mrs Prizbilski's first letter and I saw no point in bringing it all up again. Is that answer enough for you?'

Clare looked at him and felt something harden within her. 'No,' she said shortly. 'I don't think it is any more. I'm quite sure that those are only excuses, and that you were thinking only of yourself when you decided not to show me that letter. You don't want children. You never have. You're far too selfish.'

'That isn't true,' Boyd cut in. 'I admit I wasn't all that worried when we first got married, but when you decided that you wanted children I was happy to go along with it.'

'And even more happy when I lost them and you made me promise not to try again,' she shot at him.

Boyd's face whitened. 'That is a diabolical thing to say.'

'Is it? Had you convinced yourself that it was all for my sake? That you were willing to make the sacrifice to protect my health?' she jeered. 'I wonder why I don't believe you. Could it be that I know you too well?'

He made an angry gesture with his hand but managed to keep his temper in check. 'All right! I've done something you don't like and I'm sorry. Must you turn it into a full-scale row?'

'But that's the point; you're not sorry. You'd do it again if it suited you. I wonder why I haven't heard from Luc yet—or have you hidden that letter, too?'

Boyd took a furious step towards her. 'What the hell do you think I am?'

'I know exactly what you are,' Clare retorted, her voice rising. 'You're a selfish, egotistical hypocrite. You even pretend to yourself that you're doing things for my sake, when all the time you——'

'All right!' Boyd shouted. 'You don't have to spell it out; I get the message. I'm sorry I decided not to show

you the damn letter. In future I won't let my concern
for you govern my actions. Here, take it.' Striding to
the bureau, he grabbed up the letter and thrust it at her.
'You deal with it. And if she writes again don't bother
to show me; I'm sure you can handle it better than I
can.' He went to turn away but then swung back. 'And
you don't have to wait until I'm asleep before you come
creeping into bed, Clare—a simple "No" would suffice!'

He slammed out of the room, leaving Clare staring
after him. She found that she was shaking, more angry
than she'd ever been in all her life. The armchair was
near by and she almost fell into it, her legs feeling suddenly unable to support her. She felt stunned, almost as
if she'd been physically hit. This can't go on, she thought
dully. I can't live like this. She tried to think objectively,
but it was impossible; her emotions were too involved,
her thoughts chaotic.

For the rest of that weekend they hardly spoke to one
another, Clare shutting herself away in her studio while
Boyd took advantage of the fine weather to attack the
garden as if it were an enemy.

And on Monday, after Boyd had left for work even
earlier than usual, the letter from Luc Chamond arrived. An impersonal letter, typed by a secretary, confirming that he would try to arrange for some of her
pictures to be shown in Paris in May. But he had added
a postscript in his own hand:

> I was charmed to meet and talk with you. Will you
> have lunch with me again when I'm next in London?

There was no mention of her bringing more pictures
for him to see, Clare noted, but perhaps that went
without saying. She chose to think it did.

It was gone ten when Boyd got home after his French
class, although she'd expected him an hour earlier. Clare

was in the sitting-room, watching television. He came
to kiss her, as he always did, but Clare turned her head
away, her face set into mulish lines. Boyd became still,
then straightened up without having touched her, his jaw
tight. 'Good evening, darling,' he said sardonically.
'Have you had a good day?'

She threw him a look and got to her feet. 'Do you
want anything to eat?' she asked ungraciously.

'Don't bother; I'll get it myself.'

She didn't argue, just sat down again and went on
watching the programme. Boyd went into the kitchen
and presently she smelt the savoury aroma of soup and
warm bread. On other occasions such as this, when Boyd
had come home late and made himself something, he
had always brought it into the sitting-room on a tray so
that he could talk to her while he ate, but tonight he
stayed in the kitchen, eating at the table in there. When
the programme ended Clare switched off the set and went
upstairs to have her bath. There was no knock on the
door tonight, no offer to wash her back.

Boyd was already in bed, sitting up and reading by
the light of the lamp when she went into the bedroom.
Clare took off her dressing-gown and got into bed.
'Goodnight,' she said shortly, and turned her back towards him.

He put out the light and slid down in bed. For a few
moments there was no sound in the room, just a taut,
prickly silence. Clare lay tensely, ready for instant re-
jection if he tried to touch her. But then Boyd sighed
and said, 'Goodnight, my darling,' and turned on to his
side, away from her.

Clare received several phone calls during the next two
weeks: surreptitious ones from Melanie, who said that
she'd promised Peter she wouldn't call, but still asking
for advice and encouragement, and belligerent ones from

Angie, reporting on Ian's continuing lack of support.
Forcing herself to listen, Clare realised that she was the
last person they ought to turn to if they only knew it.
She and Boyd had had disagreements before in their
seven-year marriage, but nothing had ever been as bad
as it was now. Boyd continued to come home late, often
after she had gone to bed, and he didn't ask her about
her work or talk about his any more. At the weekend
they had friends round to dinner and managed to bury
their differences in a shallow grave for a few hours, but
when their guests had left Boyd turned on the disc player
and listened to it in a brooding silence, not coming to
bed until the early hours. Clare pretended to be asleep,
but by now she was beginning to feel lonely and blamed
Boyd for the widening gap between them.

It was during this period of tension that Luc came to
London again. Clare didn't hesitate to accept his invitation to lunch, and she deliberately didn't tell Boyd,
travelling up to town by train. This time she met Luc at
his hotel. She enquired for him at the desk and when
she had given her name was directed to the bar, where
he was waiting for her. He stood politely to greet her
and ask her how she was. They chatted for a while over
a drink, but then he looked at his watch and said, 'I
hope you don't mind if we eat in the hotel. There is an
auction today and there are one or two lots I am
interested in, so I have arranged with the auction house
to call me here so that I can make my bids by telephone.'

'Of course not,' Clare agreed, thinking how cosmo-
politan Luc sounded.

They finished their drinks and Luc led her out of the
bar, but instead of going towards the restaurant he
headed for the lifts. She hesitated looking up at him un-
certainly. 'Aren't we going to eat in the restaurant?'

'No, I have arranged for the meal to be served in my suite. I do not want the other customers in the restaurant to overhear when I make my bids, you understand?'

'Oh, I see.'

Suddenly acutely aware of Boyd's warning, Clare almost backed out, but the lift doors opened, some other people got in, and Luc was holding his arm out, waiting for her to go in ahead of him, and somehow it was impossible not to step into it. It was a large suite with a bedroom and separate sitting-room, and she was relieved to see a table already set for lunch, a bottle of champagne beside it in an ice-bucket. A waiter arrived with the food trolley almost at once, and they had hardly started their first course before Luc received his first phone call from the auction and started bidding crisply, and coolly. Clare gave an inward sigh of relief, mentally blaming Boyd for having made her nervous, and settled down to enjoy herself.

Which she did. The food was good and it was fun to serve themselves. Between phone calls Luc set out to entertain and amuse her, paid her compliments and made her feel young and feminine. And Clare needed to feel like that, needed it badly. And because he was so much older she felt it safe to flatter him in return by flirting with him a little, a sort of repayment for making her feel so much happier, but when Luc said, 'When will you come to Paris so that I can show you my lovely city?' she immediately drew back.

'I suppose when we bring my paintings across for the exhibition.'

'We?'

'Boyd and I; he's promised to drive me over. I couldn't manage to drive to Paris on my own.'

'No, of course not,' Luc agreed, his expression just slightly disappointed, but nowhere near enough to make her wary.

'It works out very well,' Clare remarked. 'We're going to a trade fair in Bruges in April, but we'll be back in time to drive over to Paris with my paintings. How many do you think you'll want?'

'Why don't you bring as many as you have so that my partner in the gallery and I can choose?' He smiled at her. 'Will you be helping at the trade fair?'

'Not really. Boyd is the one who'll be doing all the work during the day at the fair, but I'll be acting as the hostess for all the entertaining he'll have to do in the evenings.'

'So you'll be free to explore Bruges. You're very lucky; it's a beautiful city.'

'So I've heard. I'm really looking forward to it.' Which was only partly true; in the present circumstances Clare wasn't at all sure that she wanted to go anywhere with Boyd.

'I have business interests there myself.' Luc's head came up as an idea occurred to him. 'If I can't show you Paris, why don't I show you Bruges? I have to go there before long anyway, and I can easily arrange to be there at the same time as you. That would give me great pleasure.' He touched her hand lightly. 'There are some marvellous works of art in Bruges that I would like to share with you.'

'That's awfully kind of you,' Clare answered. 'But I don't really feel that I can commit myself in case Boyd has made other plans for me.'

'Of course.' Luc gave a very Gallic shrug. 'But if you find that you are free you can always call me. It is no distance from Paris to Bruges.'

A marvellous lunch, flattering comments about the two paintings she'd taken for him to see; Clare felt in a much better mood as she came out of the hotel. She even felt ready to make up with Boyd. So much so that she bought herself a new dress in a green shade to match her eyes, a colour she knew he loved on her. It was sexy, too, low-cut at the back, clinging round the waist and hips, then swirlingly full around her knees.

Still feeling good when she got home, Clare went up to the bedroom, switched on some music and tried the dress on again to decide which pair of shoes would best go with it. Then she played around with her hair, brushing it over to one side of her head in a thick mane of chestnut curls, adding one big gold earring that hung down the length of her neck. Standing in front of the mirror, Clare looked herself over, smiling at her own reflection as she thought how good it would be to make up with Boyd.

She didn't hear him come home, was completely unaware that there was anyone else in the house until she caught sight of Boyd's reflection in the mirror as he stood in the open doorway, watching her.

She gave a startled gasp and put a hand to her mouth. 'Oh, you frightened me.'

'Maybe it's your guilty conscience working overtime again.'

She looked at him doubtfully, recognising that he was in a strange mood but unable to discern whether it was good or bad. 'You're home early,' she said cautiously.

'Yes. Had a good day? Been working hard?'

Deciding to keep things light, Clare laughed and shook her head. 'As a matter of fact, I took the day off and went up to town. And I bought this dress.' She spun around and smiled at him. 'Do you like it?'

'*You* bought it?'

'Of course.'

Boyd's mouth twisted into a sneer and his words came out like bullets. 'For whose benefit—Luc Chamond's when you met him at his hotel?'

She stared at him. 'But how did you——?'

'How did I find out?' His voice became cuttingly cold. 'I tried to phone you here several times but couldn't get any answer. It occurred to me that Chamond might be in London again, so I called the gallery—and they confirmed that he was lunching at his hotel today. So I called the hotel and asked for you. They told me that you were lunching with Chamond—in his room!'

Realising that any attempt to make up would be useless now, Clare drew herself up, her voice hardening to disguise her disappointment. 'So what?'

'So why didn't you tell me you were meeting him again?'

Turning to the mirror, she took off the earring. 'I didn't think we were on such intimate terms as actually telling one another anything. And, anyway, it doesn't concern you.'

Catching her arm, Boyd spun her round. 'It concerns me when you meet another man—especially when you're playing the virgin with me.'

'It isn't like that,' she protested.

'No? Then why the hell did you wear a dress as sexy as that unless you were willing to be seduced?'

The accusation, after the high hopes she'd had when she bought the dress, made Clare's temper erupt. 'I bought the dress *after* I met him. But it would serve you damn well right if I did let him seduce me! At least he treats me as a person, as an individual.'

Grabbing hold of her other wrist, Boyd's fingers bit deep into her flesh, hurting her. 'If you go to bed with him we're through,' he said savagely.

'That's all you care about, isn't it? Sex. You don't even think of me as a person, just as your wife, the woman you go to bed with. Your property. And if anyone else lays a finger on me then that's it—finished!'

Boyd's face tightened, his eyes angrier than she'd ever known. 'That's right,' he said fiercely. 'My property. To take when I like. And I want you now!'

Letting go of one of her wrists, he put his hand on the neck of the dress and tore it down, enjoying her gasp of horror. She struggled, hitting out at him, but was no match for his strength and anger. He caught both her wrists in one of his and bore her down on the bed, his free hand tearing at the rest of her clothes. Tears of helpless rage and humiliation came into Clare's eyes as she lay naked before him. 'You coward!' she spat at him. 'You loathsome coward.'

Boyd's hand had gone to his trouser belt, but at her words his head came up and he looked into her face, seeing the revulsion in her eyes. The fury was suddenly wiped from his features, to be replaced by paralysing shock. He didn't speak for a long moment, then, 'Dear God,' he breathed. 'What have you done to me?' Rolling off her, he quickly did up his belt, then ran from the room and down the stairs, out of the house, the door slamming behind him.

Leaving Clare lying on the bed, staring up at the ceiling. So much for love, she thought bitterly. She didn't move for a long time, but then she reached out and picked up the phone, called Luc at his hotel and said shortly, 'Circumstances have changed. I will be able to meet you in Bruges after all.'

CHAPTER EIGHT

THERE was nothing to be done with the green dress. Clare, once she'd put on jeans and a sweater, picked up the pieces of her torn clothes, took them downstairs and burnt them on the sitting-room fire. Watching the pieces of green material smoulder and burst into flame, she thought that she was watching what was left of her marriage turn into ashes, too. One thing was for sure; she couldn't live with Boyd any more. Not after what had happened this afternoon. She had never seen him so angry, so savagely violent. Had never thought him capable of such jealous rage. She shivered, frightened by the violent emotions she had unleashed, her hands still trembling as she poked the last remnants into flame.

She didn't know what to do, whether to pack a few clothes and go, or whether Boyd had walked out for good this time. It would be ridiculous if they both walked out, she thought on a high, hysterical giggle. And anyway, why should she be the one to move out? It was Boyd who had leapt to all the wrong conclusions, who hadn't trusted her. Full of hurt, and injured pride, Clare decided that *she* wasn't going anywhere. Boyd must be the one to go. Go and live with Velma the Vamp if he wanted to, for all she cared. Clare's sense of injury almost smothered the flash of jealousy that that thought brought, but not quite.

When Boyd came back she was ready to do battle again, but instead of the rage she'd expected his face was drawn and there was a defeated look in his eyes. Suddenly all the belligerence left her as Clare saw what an enormous chasm had opened between them, one that seemed impossible ever to bridge.

'Would—would you like a drink?' she asked stiffly.

He glanced at her under frowning brows, then nodded. 'Thanks.'

Clare poured the drinks and handed one to him, then went to sit in the armchair on the other side of the fireplace. It had been a mild day and she hadn't bothered to light the fire, but she would have been glad of one now, some warmth to dispel the terrible coldness between them.

Boyd took a long swallow of his drink, but when he didn't speak she said, 'What are we going to do, Boyd? We can't go on like this.'

He leaned back against the chair almost casually, but in the hand that gripped the arm the knuckles showed white. 'What do you want to do?' he answered harshly.

Painfully she said, 'Maybe we—we ought to give each other some space.'

His mouth twisted into a thin smile. 'That sounds very ambiguous. What exactly do you mean by it?'

'I thought—I thought...' Clare pushed her hair off her face, her hand trembling, finding it almost impossible to go on, to say the words that might split them apart forever. Licking lips gone dry, she forced herself to say, 'Perhaps we ought to live apart for a while.'

She could speak in no more than a mumble but Boyd heard her quite clearly. For a brief moment his face was completely desolate, but then his features hardened into a cold mask, taut with tension, and there was an unnatural hoarseness in his voice as he said, 'You want to leave?'

'Well, I thought that perhaps you could find somewhere in London and——'

'No! This is my home and I'm not going to damn well move out.'

Taken aback by his vehemence, Clare said, 'But you didn't want to leave London in the first place.'

Ignoring that, he said, 'We made this home together and I am not going to leave it to live in some impersonal hotel or bed and breakfast place.'

She hadn't thought about where he would go, only that she wanted him to leave. But there was no arguing with that kind of determination. 'Then I'll have to move out,' she said, afraid to even envisage the future.

'Does it have to be anything so drastic? Can't we try and talk it through?'

Clare shook her head sadly. 'It's to late for that. I can't—I can't live with you any more.' Her voice broke and she put up a hand to cover her eyes. 'If we don't— trust each other then there's nothing left.'

Boyd drained his glass, put it down, and gripped both the arms of the chair. 'I don't want you to leave.'

'I *have* to,' she said on a low, desperate note.

She couldn't look at him, afraid to see his face, and it was a long time before he said, in a strange, empty kind of voice, 'I can't stop you if you want to go, but I won't leave you. I'll *never* leave you.'

Her head came up at that and she gazed into his bleak, set face for a long, long moment. Then Clare nodded and slowly got up out of the chair, having to pull herself up like an old woman, her body feeling drained of strength. She held on to the banister going up the stairs and she sat on her bed, gazing into space, until at last she roused herself to find a suitcase and start packing some clothes.

When she came down again with her coat on Boyd came into the hall. 'Where will you go? To your mother's?'

She gave a mirthless laugh at that. 'No, definitely not there.'

'Where, then?'

'I don't know. I'll find somewhere.'

'Do you have enough money?'

She nodded, unable to speak.

His jaw tightened. 'You don't have to do this, Clare.'

She just looked at him, her eyes deep pools of inner pain, close to tears. Blindly she turned for the door.

'You'll let me know where you are,' Boyd said urgently. She nodded again but he caught her arm. 'You promise? You'll phone me tonight and tell me where you are?'

'Yes. I—I promise.' She dragged her arm away. 'Please let me go!' And she wrenched open the door and ran out into the night, lugging her case round to the car, throwing it in, driving away with tears pouring down her cheeks.

Clare found a room in a motel, but it was several hours later before she could find the courage to keep her promise. Boyd picked up the phone at once, as if he'd been sitting by it.

She told him where she was and he said, 'You're sure you're all right?'

'Yes.'

'Have you had something to eat?'

'I'm—I'm not hungry.'

'You must eat. Promise me you'll eat.'

'Yes, all right.'

'I'll be here,' he said, 'when you're ready to come home.'

A great lump came into her heart. 'I—I know.'

'And there are things we have to discuss, arrange. What we tell your mother, our friends. Your things;

you'll need more than you have. And what about your work? And what about the company functions you've promised to attend?'

Clare could feel her whole body harden and her voice grow bitter as she said, 'I might have known that that would be the first thing you'd think of.'

But Boyd's tone was sad as he said, 'It was by far the last thing, Clare; by far the last.'

She didn't believe him and put the phone down.

During the next couple of weeks they worked out a compromise; Clare went to the house during the day so that she could work in the studio, but she left early enough to avoid seeing Boyd. Unwilling to pay the high charges at the motel, she quickly found herself a bed-sit in the nearby town, a reasonably clean place with a bed, which was all she cared about. She had never felt so unhappy in all her life, or so lonely. It felt so strange, being alone. For all that she had been a modern career girl when she'd met Boyd, she had never lived on her own before, going straight from living at home with her mother to marriage with Boyd. There had been no period of independence and self-sufficiency in between. There had always been someone else to rely on, to share things with.

She missed Boyd with a deep ache that was like a pain, and she was infinitely miserable alone at night in the unfamiliar room. But this, she knew, was probably what Boyd had intended when he'd refused so adamantly to move out. He wanted to wear her down by the loss of all that they had worked for, as much as anything else. Contrarily, knowing this hardened Clare's resolve. She would prove to herself that she could be independent, that she could lead her own life the way she wanted to.

The only person she told was Angie when they had the stall at the antiques fair, and to her surprise, expecting a sympathetic hearer, found instead that her friend was terribly shocked, even angry.

'You've got to go back to him,' Angie said forcefully. 'You two are made for each other. And Boyd doesn't deserve that you should do this to him.'

They argued and both got a little heated, but then the customers crowded in as the doors were opened, and they were relieved to be able to concentrate on the stall, Clare wishing heartily that she hadn't said anything.

There was one company dinner that she had to attend with Boyd, both of them pretending like mad that everything was fine, but when they came out of the restaurant Clare went immediately to her own car and drove away, while Boyd walked more slowly to his. The next occasion was the trade fair in Bruges. She didn't even try to get out of this one, but, when they talked about it on the phone, insisted that Boyd book her into a separate hotel.

'Don't be silly,' he said shortly. 'Everyone from the company is booked into the same hotel.'

'Then I'm not going. I'm not going to share a room with you.'

She could imagine the flame of anger that would come into his eyes at that, but there was nothing Boyd could say, not after the way he'd almost taken her against her will on the night of their last huge row. 'How about if I book a suite with two bedrooms—with locks on the doors, of course?' he added sardonically. 'Will that satisfy you?'

'Yes, I suppose so. But I want the days free. I can't act as if nothing has happened for twenty-four hours a day.'

'All right, if that's what you want.'

She was surprised that he'd given in so easily, had expected to have to fight more than that, and was strangely disquieted by it.

On the day they were due to leave, Clare drove over to the house and they travelled to Bruges together, both observing an unspoken and uneasy kind of truce, but the tension high between them. When they arrived, in the early afternoon, Boyd went straight to the centre where the fair was being held, and, with nothing better to do, Clare went with him. Velma the Vamp was there. Looking assured and sophisticated in a well-cut suit with a short skirt that showed off her long, shapely legs. They greeted each other politely, but Clare saw from the malicious pleasure in Velma's face that she knew that she and Boyd had split up.

There was a cocktail party that night, given by the organisers of the fair, and the next day she went walking round Bruges alone. It was a beautiful city, all and more than she had expected, her artistic eye being delighted at every turn, but Clare was too absorbed in her own problems to really enjoy it. Sometimes she thought that she would never enjoy anything again.

Luc arrived in Bruges the next day. Clare hadn't told Boyd he was coming. She told herself it was because what she did was no longer Boyd's business, but really it was because she was afraid to tell him, afraid it would lead to another row.

They'd arranged to meet outside the town hall, in the big square where the horse-drawn carriages waited for hire. Luc was waiting and seemed very pleased to see her; his smiling face was a welcome change after the brooding tension between her and Boyd. 'The only way to really see Bruges is to walk,' he told her. 'So this morning we will walk and this afternoon we will look at pictures, yes?'

'Fine,' Clare agreed, and didn't object when he tucked her arm in his.

Luc was as good a guide as he was a conversationalist, and Clare tried to be as good a companion, but her heart wasn't really in it. Only when they went to the Groeninge Museum to look at the magnificent paintings there was she able to forget for a blissful few hours. 'Will you have dinner with me this evening?' Luc asked as they came out.

'I'm sorry, but I can't. I have to be at a dinner party Boyd's company is giving this evening.'

'Till tomorrow, then. Same time and place?'

'Thank you. I'd like that very much.'

The evening, in contrast to her peaceful day with Luc, soon became almost a battlefield. Clare was supposed to be the hostess at the party, but Velma, in a low-cut silver lamé dress, was determined to be the centre of attention, going up to greet people before Clare had a chance to, calling the waiter over to hand out drinks, being over-vivacious—and putting a familiar hand on Boyd's arm when they stood together, talking to some of the guests. Her performance made Clare feel sick, but she didn't feel that she had the right to do anything about it; by walking out on Boyd she had forfeited that right. It was a relief when the party was over and they got back to the hotel.

'Fancy a drink in the bar?' Boyd asked.

She shook her head. 'No, I think I'll go straight up.'

'As you wish.' He turned as Velma and some other men from the company arrived. Velma gave him a dazzling smile and gathered him up with her as they all went into the bar.

Clare listened for a long time but didn't hear Boyd come into the suite, wasn't sure that he came to his bedroom at all that night.

She was poor company the next morning as she and Luc explored the city, and over lunch Clare found herself telling him that she had left Boyd. He was very sympathetic, very encouraging, telling her that she had done the right thing, that she had a great future before her as an artist. His was the only voice that didn't condemn what she'd done, the only one who was on her side. Clare was so grateful and so relieved to talk to someone who understood that she couldn't help crying a little.

'You are in no mood to look at pictures this afternoon,' Luc declared. 'Come, I know a place where we can go.'

He took her to an apartment in an old building overlooking the canal. It was furnished with antiques in a rather sombre style but there were some good paintings on the walls. Luc mixed her a drink and sat beside her on the high-backed settee. 'Drink this,' he instructed. 'It will make you feel better.'

It tasted pretty strong and went to her head a little, especially after the wine they'd had at lunch, but Clare didn't much care. She thought that she wouldn't ever care about anything any more.

She found she did when the comforting arm that Luc had put round her shoulders tightened and he drew her to him. 'My poor little one. Why don't you let me take care of you? I can give you so much more. I understand the kind of background an artist like you needs. And I can help you. Help you.' He began to kiss her neck and his hand went to her breast.

For a moment Clare was so astounded by what was happening that she didn't react, but then she gave an exclamation of horror and tried to push him away. But Luc's arms tightened around her as he pushed her back againt the settee and leant against her, his mouth avidly seeking hers.

'Don't! Stop it.' She struggled to push him away but was held within the circle of his arms, arms that were far more powerful than she could have imagined.

'I want you, Clare.' His breath was hot against her cheek as she turned her face away from his kisses. 'You won't be sorry. I'm a good lover. Very experienced.'

'No!' With a sudden, violent movement she slid down through his arms and ducked under them, her hair swirling as she jumped up off the settee.

Luc, too, jumped to his feet and looked as if he was coming after her, his arms outstretched.

'Keep away from me,' she yelled at him, and grabbed up a poker from the fireplace.

He stopped, an astounded look on his face, then raised his palms towards her. 'Gently. There is no need for this hysteria. I was only trying to comfort you.'

'No, you damn well weren't!'

He looked at her angry face for a moment, then shrugged. 'Very well, I admit I wanted you. Is that so bad?'

'Yes. It is,' she retorted shortly. 'You're old, old enough to be my father.'

Luc flinched but said in a cold voice, 'Why else do you think I have bothered to spend time with you?'

'I thought you were interested in me as an artist. As a friend.'

He laughed. 'An artist?' He laughed again, the jeering, derisive sound of it warning her what was to come. 'You're a hack and you'll never be anything more. A real artist would be ashamed to have his pictures shown on the same walls as yours.'

Clare's face whitened. She didn't speak but went to pick up her bag from the floor near the settee. As she did so Luc caught her arm. Looking intently into her eyes, he said, 'I am not offering you just a one-night stand. You can stay here in this apartment. In this beautiful city. You have left your husband; where else do you have to go? You would find me very generous, Clare, very appreciative.'

She gazed back at him and said slowly, 'And my paintings?'

'We would show them, of course,' he said smoothly. 'I was angry before. I can make you famous.'

The casting-couch syndrome; Clare remembered Boyd's warning and her mouth thinned into a painful smile. Seeing it, Luc thought he'd won, and his eyes glistened triumphantly. Shaking him off, Clare said, 'My husband was right about you; he always said you were a dirty old man.' Then she turned and strode away.

She didn't go straight back to the hotel but wandered around for a long time. It was much cooler and windy today; the breeze blew her hair around her head, hiding the tears that came to her eyes. At five, the time the fair closed, Clare went back to the hotel. Boyd was already there. Waiting in the small sitting-room between the bedrooms, a drink in his hand. When she came in she realised at once that he was terribly angry, but the anger was suppressed into an ice-cold inner rage.

Without preamble he said, 'Velma went out on an errand for me this morning. She came back and said that she had seen you with a man. A suave-looking middle-aged man.'

A pain of agony went through Clare's heart at the inevitability of it all, but she merely said, 'Yes, it was Luc,' and walked into her bedroom.

It took only a few minutes to pack. Boyd was still sitting there. She didn't say anything, didn't try to prolong it, just walked past him and out of the door.

*   *   *

They didn't meet or even speak again for a couple of weeks. Clare didn't go to the house to work; it wasn't necessary, because she gave up painting. Instead she found a job in a small business that made Christmas-tree decorations, sticking coloured sequins on to poly-styrene shapes. Then Boyd rang her at the bed-sit one evening. 'It's your husband,' the landlady called up to her.

Running down to the hall, Clare nervously picked up the receiver. 'Hello?'

'Your sister-in-law rang,' Boyd said shortly. 'It seems you promised to look after the boys for a weekend. She and Derek have been invited to spend this weekend on a friend's boat as the weather looks to be good, and she wants to know if it will be OK for us to have the boys.'

'Did you tell her about—about us?'

'No.'

'I can't have them here. I—I'll ring her and tell her we're busy.'

'It's too late for that. I told her to bring them over.'

'But you can't! I couldn't possibly——'

'Why should they be disappointed?' Boyd cut in sharply. 'I've already told her that you'll be here to look after them. She's bringing them over on Friday evening— *so be here.*' And he put down the phone.

The weather was good that week; Clare could just see the sun through the skylight of the old warehouse-type building she was working in. She drove straight from work over to the house, wanting to be sure that she was there before Christina turned up with the children. There were beds to be made up, too, not only for her nephews but also for herself; she couldn't bring herself to sleep in their marriage bed, even if Boyd wasn't there—it would hold too many memories. She hadn't expected

Boyd to be at the house, but he was; he'd been shopping and was loading food into the fridge.

He glanced up as she came in but then went on with his task, saying, 'I'm afraid I'm not up-to-date on what little boys eat, but I've bought fish-fingers, beefburgers, chips, and a lot of cans of Coke.'

'You'll be their friend for life,' Clare said lightly. 'Although I think it would be better if you didn't tell Christina.'

He gave a short laugh. 'No, I suppose not.' And stood up.

She hadn't expected him to be here and didn't know what to expect now they'd met again, how he would react. Whether it would immediately become a battle-field or whether he wouldn't even speak to her. But it seemed it was to be neither of those things—at least, not yet. Her eyes searched his face, seeing there the tell-tale lines of strain around his mouth and eyes. Lines that she had seen mirrored in her own face after each sleepless night.

'It was good of you to get the food,' she said, treading carefully. 'I was going to take them with me to the supermarket this evening.'

'I was able to get away from work early.' He stuck his hands in his pockets. 'There's a film on they might like; I thought perhaps we could all go tonight.'

A hammer began to pound in Clare's chest. 'You're staying.'

'Yes.'

'You—you don't have to.' Realising how that sounded, Clare said quickly, 'It's not that I don't want you to, it's just—you don't *have* to. If you've got other things you'd rather do. Someone else you'd—rather be with,' she added painfully.

'I know what you meant. I'm staying.'

Clare could only nod and say, 'Right. I—er—I'll take my things up.'

In the nursery—the room that they had intended to be the nursery—the twin beds had already been neatly made up with sheets, pillows and duvets. Boyd had been busy. And in the third bedroom, the guest room, the bed had also been made up. For her, presumably, so she needn't have worried. Feeling like a guest in her own home, Clare unpacked the few things she'd brought with her and went downstairs again. As she did so her brother and his family arrived, the boys—Simon, the elder, who was five, and Ben, aged three—bursting out of the car, each clutching an overnight bag stuffed with toys.

There was no time then for nervous tension, no time to be alone with Boyd. The parents left, they gave the boys some food and then went to the cinema, much to the boys' delight; it seemed they had never been in the evening before. With the boys sitting between them there was no opportunity to even speak at the cinema, and they weren't alone until the children had eventually been bathed, put to bed, read to, and at last fallen asleep.

Clare came downstairs and dropped into a chair. 'Phew! I can't imagine how Christina copes.'

'They're excited tonight.' Boyd gave her a drink and sat opposite her. 'What shall we do with them tomorrow?'

'I don't know. Have you got anything in mind?'

'There's the open-air museum. They've got an old mine-shaft you can go down. The boys might like that.'

'If it means they can get dirty I'm sure they would,' Clare remarked.

Boyd grinned at that and she smiled tentatively back, almost afraid to do so. She had expected him to ask about Luc and couldn't understand why he didn't. Or why he was staying. And why he wasn't still angry.

'Do you really want to come with us tomorrow?'

'Are you trying to say that you don't want me?' Boyd said levelly.

'No, of course not,' she said quickly. 'It's just that—well, I thought you might want to go out with Velma.'

Boyd's eyebrows rose. 'I have never wanted to go anywhere with Velma. Why should you think so?'

'She was out to get you,' Clare said baldly. 'She made that perfectly clear. You took her to Milan and didn't tell me, and you bought her a present. She—she flaunted it at me.'

'If I didn't tell you it was because it was unimportant. And it's usual to give your secretary a present on her birthday.' He looked at her. 'But that isn't all?'

'No. When—when we were in Bruges she kept touching you all the time, as if she had the right to do so. As if you were lovers.'

'We were never lovers,' Boyd said in a tone that made her instantly believe him. 'But I know what you mean, and that's why I had her transferred to another department.'

'You did?' Clare's eyes opened wide.

'Yes, but she didn't like it, so she's leaving.'

Clare didn't know what to say to that and quickly finished her drink and stood up. 'I'm tired. Goodnight.'

'Goodnight, Clare.' Boyd's voice sounded rather wry behind her.

The next day was a good one, at the museum where they had a picnic, and later in the evening at the river, where Boyd hired a boat and they took it in turns to row, stopped at a pub for drinks all round, and then had to light the boat's lamp as Boyd rowed them back in the dark, the boys' excited voices echoing across the water.

'I do like it here, Auntie Clare,' Simon said as she put him to bed that night. Putting his arms round her neck, he gave her a warm, wet kiss. 'You and Uncle Boyd will let us come again, won't you?'

'Yes, of course,' Clare answered with a catch in her throat.

'You promise?'

'I promise.'

Satisfied, he slid into bed. Ben was already asleep; they were too tired for a story tonight. She sat for a while, watching them even after Simon had fallen asleep. So long that Boyd came up to find her.

'Are you all right?' he asked from the open doorway.

Rousing herself, Clare nodded and got to her feet. She didn't have to say anything; he knew from the sadness in her eyes what she'd been thinking. They went out on to the landing, leaving the door carefully ajar in case one of the children should wake.

'Come down and have a drink,' Boyd invited and went to lead the way downstairs.

But Clare shook her head. Looking at him, she said, 'I'm—I'm sorry, Boyd.'

She wasn't talking about the drink and they both knew it. Boyd started to say, 'Clare——' but she turned and hurried to her room, closing the door firmly behind her.

Sunday was another gloriously hot day, more like summer than spring. Boyd took the boys swimming in the morning and they had a barbecue at lunchtime, the boys insisting on helping Boyd to cook, large aprons tied round their tiny waists. He patiently explained what to do, making sure they didn't burn themselves, so that Clare, watching him, thought again what a wonderful father he would have made, even if he didn't realise it himself. After the meal she dished out ice-cream for the children and then wandered down the garden to lean against the apple tree, its branches thick with buds about to burst into blossom.

Boyd followed her and put a hand on the trunk near her shoulder. 'It's been good, this weekend,' he said.

She smiled. 'I suppose we're rather in the position of grandparents, and the kids are all right because we can give them back.'

'Perhaps.' He put his hand on her shoulder, bare above her sun-top. 'Be careful you don't burn.'

She nodded, unable to look at him, her heart thumping, and her skin electric beneath his hand. She wanted to tell him about Luc, that they hadn't been lovers, but then thought, what was the use? The basic differences were still there and he hadn't trusted her.

'Clare?' He was looking at her intently, searching her face. 'Clare, I think we have to——'

A shrill, frightened scream cut through his words and they both jerked round. It was Ben, his hands up to his face. He began to scream again and they both ran to him. 'What is it? What's happened?'

But Ben's mouth was wide open as he went on screaming, tears of terror on his ice-cream-stained cheeks.

'It was an insect,' Simon shrilled. 'A big one. It stung him.'

'Oh, no!' Clare caught hold of Ben and tried to pull his hands down so that she could see his face.

'Was it a wasp or a bee?' Boyd demanded.

'I don't know, I didn't see properly.'

Boyd picked up Ben and they ran into the kitchen. 'Some vinegar,' he said. 'That helps.'

Clare flew to get it and Boyd bathed it on the child's face, talking soothingly as he did so. Ben stopped screaming but he began to pant, his breathing laboured. 'Is he hysterical, do you think?'

'I don't know.' Boyd frowned and took Ben's pulse.

'His face is starting to swell. But I can't see any sting. Bees always leave them behind, don't they?' she said worriedly.

'Clare, I don't like the look of this. I think he may have an allergic reaction. Let's get him to hospital.' She stared, consumed by horror, until Boyd said urgently, 'Come on, darling. Let's *move*.'

She burst into action then, grabbing Simon and an overcoat that hung on the back of the kitchen door, locking up the house as Boyd ran out to the car. She got in the back with Simon and wrapped the coat round Ben as Boyd handed him to her. Then Boyd got in the car, said tersely, 'Hang on,' and drove as he never had before.

Unaware of any real danger to his brother, Simon thoroughly enjoyed their mad dash to the hospital, Boyd using all his skill and breaking every speed limit in his new car. Clare could only sit in the back and silently urge him on as she saw Ben's skin start to turn blue. Boyd braked sharply outside the casualty department, but Clare had the door open and was out of the car almost before he'd stopped. They ran inside, calling for help, and a nurse immediately came forward. Within moments Ben was taken from them and had been whisked away. In seconds they had gone from a dizzy eighty miles an hour to standing still with nothing to do but wait.

'Auntie Clare? Uncle Boyd?' Simon's hands went into theirs and they looked down at his anxious face.

Boyd bent to pick him up. 'I think we'd better go and move the car.'

Clare found that she was trembling, but couldn't sit down, could only lean against the wall, her eyes fixed on the door through which Ben had been rushed. He was so little, so little. When Boyd came back, holding

Simon's hand, he didn't attempt to get her to sit down, just put his arm round her and held her tightly against him, giving them both the comfort of his strength.

A nurse came up to them. 'Are you the little boy's parents?'

'No, he's our nephew,' Boyd answered, and gave her all the particulars she wanted.

They were left alone then until the senior nurse came to find them. Clare looked at her in terrified anxiety, but the nurse smiled, she actually smiled, and Clare felt faint with relief. Boyd's arm tightened and it was he who talked to the nurse.

'Ben is going to be fine. But it's a good job you brought him in straight away. He went into anaphylactic shock. Did you know he would react like that?'

'No,' Boyd admitted. 'I imagine he's never been stung before.'

'Well, tell his parents they'll have to be careful with him in future.' She gestured through the door. 'You can come and see him, but we'll be keeping him in overnight for observation.'

Ben gave them a weak smile and they stood by his bed, reassuring him until he fell asleep, his thumb in his mouth. When they got in the car to go home Simon said, 'Drive like you did on the way here, Uncle Boyd. It was great.' And they both burst into relieved, slightly hysterical laughter.

Derek and Christina weren't due to pick up the children until the next day, so they put Simon to bed, then went and sat on the settee. Boyd put his arms round her and she leaned close to him, still trembling a little.

'It's OK,' he said softly, his mouth against her hair. 'He's going to be fine.'

'Derek would have killed me if anything had happened to Ben.' Boyd laughed softly but his arms

tightened. 'They'll never let us look after them again.'
Then she remembered. 'Not that we will anyway.'

'Why not? I think it's a very good idea.'

She lifted her head to look at him and suddenly the
words came quite easily. 'Boyd, I was never—unfaithful
to you with Luc. You were right; he did try to make love
to me, but I wouldn't let him.' Her voice became bitter.
'And you were right about him not really being interested
in my work. That was just a lure; he never intended to
show them. I think that even if I'd—done what he
wanted, he wouldn't have shown them. He fooled me,
fooled me into thinking that I'd found someone who
was interested in me just for myself.' She looked again
at Boyd. 'I truly wasn't unfaithful, Boyd.'

'I know.'

'You do? How?'

He gave a rueful laugh. 'When you walked out that
night I thought that you'd gone to him. I found that I
couldn't stand the pictures that conjured up in my mind,
so I looked up his address in the phone book and went
round there to get you back. But you weren't there.
Unfortunately I didn't find that out until I'd—er—let
him know how I felt.'

Her eyes widened. 'Boyd! You didn't hit him?'

'I might have pushed him around a little,' he conceded.

'Good. I'm glad.'

That made him laugh; his arm tightened around her
and he said, 'Your paintings are good, I don't have to
tell you that. And there are other places where you can
hold an exhibition; I don't know why we haven't thought
of it before.'

'Thanks for the moral support,' Clare said huskily.
But then she looked away. 'Maybe one day.'

Putting his hand under her chin, Boyd made her look
at him. His eyes were full of yearning, of love as he

looked into hers. 'Come back to me, darling,' he said simply. 'On any terms you want. My life is nothing without you.'

For a long moment she didn't answer, and the hope in his eyes began to die, and then she leaned forward and kissed him lightly but lingeringly on the mouth. 'Or mine,' she whispered. He gave a deep sigh of contentment and pulled her on to his lap, held her close against him, happy just to hold her in his arms, to feel her warmth against his, to know that she had come back to him. Clare cried a little and he kissed away her tears, stroked her hair.

'We're OK,' he said soothingly. 'We came through it. Nothing can come between us now because we know that anything is better than being apart. We'll work things out. We'll make sure that nothing like this ever threatens us again.'

She hugged him tightly. 'Oh, Boyd, I *do* love you.'

'Likewise, Mrs Russell,' he smiled. Putting his hands on either side of her head, he kissed her deeply. 'If you only knew how much I've missed you.'

It was Clare's turn to smile. 'I've an idea you're about to show me.'

'Yes?'

'Definitely, yes.'

He stood up, lifting her with him, and grinned, all the old love and devilment back in his face. 'You know,' he said, carrying her towards the stairs, 'I think it would be a good idea if we took a holiday.'

'Oh, so do I. A marvellous idea. Where shall we go? Somewhere hot and exotic? How about Mexico? Or the Caribbean? Or, tell you what—how about Bali? It's supposed to be beautiful there. Can we afford Bali?'

Boyd had reached the top of the stairs. 'Possibly, but I had somewhere else in mind.'

'Oh, where's that?'

He turned into their bedroom. 'Actually, I was thinking of Poland.'

'Poland!' Clare stared at him in stunned surprise. Then her eyes filled with hope. 'Oh, Boyd, you don't mean…?'

He nodded. 'I thought we'd go and find out if adoption is possible and then perhaps take a look to——' He broke off as Clare flung her arms round his neck and hugged him fiercely. 'Hey! You're strangling me, woman,' he choked. 'Stop it.' But then she began to kiss him compulsively and he fell back on the bed with her still in his arms. 'OK, go ahead,' he told her, surrendering. 'I know when I'm beaten. I'll just have to lie here and take it.'

Which he did.

Next Month's Romances

Each month you can choose from a wide variety of romance with Mills & Boon. Below are the new titles to look out for next month, why not ask either Mills & Boon Reader Service or your Newsagent to reserve you a copy of the titles you want to buy — just tick the titles you would like and either post to Reader Service or take it to any Newsagent and ask them to order your books.

Please save me the following titles:	Please tick	✓
BACHELOR AT HEART	Roberta Leigh	
TIDEWATER SEDUCTION	Anne Mather	
SECRET ADMIRER	Susan Napier	
THE QUIET PROFESSOR	Betty Neels	
ONE-NIGHT STAND	Sandra Field	
THE BRUGES ENGAGEMENT	Madeleine Ker	
AND THEN CAME MORNING	Daphne Clair	
AFTER ALL THIS TIME	Vanessa Grant	
CONFRONTATION	Sarah Holland	
DANGEROUS INHERITANCE	Stephanie Howard	
A MAN FOR CHRISTMAS	Annabel Murray	
DESTINED TO LOVE	Jennifer Taylor	
AN IMAGE OF YOU	Liz Fielding	
TIDES OF PASSION	Sally Heywood	
DEVIL'S DREAM	Nicola West	
HERE COMES TROUBLE	Debbie Macomber	

If you would like to order these books in addition to your regular subscription from Mills & Boon Reader Service please send £1.70 per title to: Mills & Boon Reader Service, P.O. Box 236, Croydon, Surrey, CR9 3RU, quote your Subscriber No:... (If applicable) and complete the name and address details below. Alternatively, these books are available from many local Newsagents including W.H.Smith, J.Menzies, Martins and other paperback stockists from 4th December 1992.

Name:...
Address:...
....Post Code:.......................

To Retailer: If you would like to stock M&B books please contact your regular book/magazine wholesaler for details.

You may be mailed with offers from other reputable companies as a result of this application. If you would rather not take advantage of these opportunities please tick box ☐

An irresistible offer from Mills & Boon

Here's a personal invitation from Mills & Boon Reader Service, to become a regular reader of Romances. To welcome you, we'd like you to have 4 books, a CUDDLY TEDDY and a special MYSTERY GIFT absolutely FREE.

Then you could look forward each month to receiving 6 brand new Romances, delivered to your door, postage and packing free! Plus our free Newsletter featuring author news, competitions, special offers and much more.

This invitation comes with no strings attached. You may cancel or suspend your subscription at any time, and still keep your free books and gifts.

It's so easy. Send no money now. Simply fill in the coupon below and post it to -
Reader Service, FREEPOST, PO Box 236, Croydon, Surrey CR9 9EL.

NO STAMP REQUIRED

Free Books Coupon

Yes! Please rush me 4 free Romances and 2 free gifts! Please also reserve me a Reader Service subscription. If I decide to subscribe I can look forward to receiving 6 brand new Romances each month for just £10.20, postage and packing free. If I choose not to subscribe I shall write to you within 10 days - I can keep the books and gifts whatever I decide. I may cancel or suspend my subscription at any time. I am over 18 years of age.

Ms/Mrs/Miss/Mr_____ EP31R

Address _____

_____

Postcode_____Signature _____

Offer expires 31st May 1993. The right is reserved to refuse an application and change the terms of this offer. Readers overseas and in Eire please send for details. Southern Africa write to Book Services International Ltd, P.O. Box 42564, Craighall, Transvaal 2024. You may be mailed with offers from other reputable companies as a result of this application.
If you would prefer not to share in this opportunity, please tick box ☐